Murder at Drumshee

Drumshee Timeline Series
Book 10

Cora Harrison

WOLFHOUND PRESS

First published in 2000 by
Wolfhound Press Ltd
68 Mountjoy Square
Dublin 1, Ireland
Tel: (353-1) 874 0354
Fax: (353-1) 872 0207

The Arts Council
An Chomhairle Ealaíon
Wolfhound Press receives financial assistance from The Arts Council/An Chomhairle Ealaíon, Dublin, Ireland.

British Library Cataloguing in Publication Data
A catalogue record for this book is available from the British Library.

ISBN 0-86327-832-9

10 9 8 7 6 5 4 3 2 1

Cover Illustration: Peter Gibson
Cover Design: Wolfhound Press
Map: Aileen Caffrey
Line Drawings: Ann Fallon
Typesetting: Wolfhound Press
Printed in the UK by Cox & Wyman Ltd, Reading, Berks.

Map of Drumshee and its Surroundings

Chapter One ❧

'I 'll kill him,' said Mahon.

The other six students from the Drumshee law school stood around awkwardly. They had been searching for Mahon for the last quarter of an hour, and now they didn't know what to say to him. He was standing under a big ash tree, his back turned to them and his arms hooked over a low branch. His face was hidden in his arms, but they could hear from his voice that he had been crying.

'He's a swine,' said Cathal at last, his face almost as red as his shock of flaming hair.

'He had no right to beat you like that just because you forgot some of the honour-prices,' said Ninian quietly.

'He seems to be worse than ever, these days,' said Diarmuid, his blue eyes full of sympathy. 'You're having a real bad time of it this week,' he added.

'It's because your father's away, Ita,' said Fergal. 'He isn't so bad when the brehon is here.'

'I suppose not,' said Ita doubtfully, chewing the end of one of her black plaits thoughtfully. Her father, Flann, was in charge of the Drumshee law school, but he was also the brehon — the lawyer — for all the district of the Burren along the west coast of Ireland; and he was away on the King's business so much that Gabur, his assistant, did what he wished with the boys. That morning he had beaten Mahon

7

savagely. Mahon had run out of the schoolhouse, and they had eventually found him under the ash tree, beside the shrine of the goddess Brigid.

'I'll talk to my father when he comes back,' Ita said resolutely. This couldn't go on, she knew that. Mahon couldn't help having a bad memory, and the continual beatings were only making him worse.

'It's no good,' said Mahon despairingly, lifting his head and running his hands through his rough, curly brown hair. He clenched and unclenched his fists. 'I can't learn all this stuff. I can't even remember whether a blacksmith is worth two and a half ounces of silver or an ounce and a half. I wish my father had never got the idea of making me a lawyer.'

The others were silent. It was true: all the knowledge which they chanted gaily, almost without thinking, Mahon found virtually impossible to learn.

'But you're not stupid,' said Fergal, a thoughtful look on his small dark face. 'You're really good at chess. You beat us all at chess; you're even better than Ita, and she's been playing with her father since she was about two years old.'

That was a nice thing to say, thought Ita. Fergal is so nice, and so sensible, too. It's true: Mahon isn't stupid, he just has a bad memory.

He was beginning to look a bit better. He had unclenched his fists, and his face was less flushed. In a while they might be able to coax him to come back to the schoolhouse and allow old Fionnuala, who looked after the boys, to put some soothing ointment on his back.

'What about a game of hurley?' asked Cathal doubtfully. Cathal was mad on hurley. Mahon made no reply, and Ita shook her head firmly at Cathal.

Ita looked at Diarmuid. He was a tall, good-looking boy with intensely blue eyes, the leader of the students at the law school. He was fifteen; the other boys were only fourteen, and she herself was only thirteen.

'Diarmuid,' she began; but Aidan interrupted her. It was a pity he was there, she thought afterwards. He was a great joker and the best fun of them all, but he wasn't the sort of person you wanted to have around when you were in trouble.

'Look, Mahon,' he said. 'There he goes!'

They all followed the direction of his pointing finger. The tall, heavy figure of Gabur, the assistant brehon, was striding down the laneway. His burly body was dressed in his newest saffron tunic, and his cloak was trimmed with pine-marten fur.

'Look at the style of him!' continued Aidan, combing his own dark fringe with his fingers and smirking in a way that made them all giggle. 'He's off to see his sweetheart — he's off to see Nessa. Look at him, Mahon! Why don't you sling a stone at him? You'll easily hit him; you're great with your sling. You can run away afterwards. We'll all swear that we don't know where you are.'

Mahon picked up a stone, his face dark with anger.

'Don't, Mahon,' said Fergal quickly. 'Don't be stupid, Aidan. He'd know it was Mahon, and there'd be no saving him then.'

'Drop that stone, Mahon,' said Diarmuid, catching his wrist. 'Drop it. You could kill a man with a stone like that. Cathal, help me to hold him!' he shouted, as Mahon struggled violently.

Cathal jumped up to help, and Mahon, glad of an

excuse to get rid of some of his temper, promptly kicked him. Cathal gave a shriek of fury and butted his red head into Mahon's stomach. Mahon went down like a log. Fergal sat on his chest, Diarmuid and Cathal held his wrists flat against the grass, and Ninian worked the stone free from his grasp and rolled it away into a nearby ditch.

Ita looked on philosophically, tossing her long black plaits back over her shoulders. The boys were always fighting. She was used to it. They would all be friends again in a few minutes. The important thing was that Mahon hadn't been allowed to do anything stupid.

'You're a birdbrain,' she said scathingly to Aidan.

'I was only joking,' he said lamely, but he gave a rather worried glance at the size of the stone that Mahon had snatched up.

'Get off me,' grunted Mahon.

Fergal looked at Diarmuid, who nodded. 'Yes, get off him. He's probably sore enough anyway, without your weight on top of him.'

Fergal got off cautiously, keeping a wary eye on Mahon. Diarmuid and Fergal loosened their grip and stood up.

Mahon lay there for a minute with his eyes closed. He does look rather white, thought Ita; he looks sick. She reached out and touched the sleeve of his tunic, her dark-green eyes full of sympathy.

'Mahon ...' she began, but he shook off her hand.

'Leave me alone, all of you,' he bellowed. Painfully, he pulled himself to his feet and set off at a shambling run towards the townland of Ballycasheen, to the north of Drumshee.

'He's gone for the day now,' said Fergal. 'He's got

some sort of hiding-place over there. I don't know where it is. Do you, Cathal?'

Cathal shook his head.

'I followed him one day,' said Aidan. 'Remember when Gabur beat him for not knowing the fine for a secret killing? I kept dodging behind the bushes and I thought I'd find it easily, but he suddenly disappeared. I asked him about it afterwards, but he just got into a temper with me.'

There was another silence as they all thought about the many beatings that Mahon had endured at Gabur's hands.

'Does he go home, do you think?' asked Ninian eventually. 'His home is somewhere over that way, I think.'

Ita shook her head. 'No,' she said. 'He doesn't go home, I'm sure of that. He told me that his father doesn't welcome him. He's disappointed that Mahon is getting on so badly at law school, after all the silver he paid for his training. He told Mahon that he doesn't want to see him again until he's a lawyer. The farm is for the other two brothers.'

'He'll never be a lawyer while Gabur's here,' said Fergal thoughtfully. 'Gabur has only to look at Mahon and every little bit of knowledge goes out of his head. Remember, Ita, when you taught Mahon that a *bóaire*, a rich farmer, has an honour-price of two and a half cows, and an *ócaire*, a small farmer, has an honour-price of one and a half cows? He knew it perfectly, because you made him imagine the farmers with their cows, and Aidan was joking about the half-cows with two legs. But the minute he went into the schoolhouse and Gabur asked him that very question, the answer just went right out of his head.'

Ita nodded. 'I know,' she said. 'And remember a few months ago, when Gabur's father died so suddenly and Gabur went to stay with his brother Colm for a few days, and Owen was our teacher? Owen taught us all to read and write Ogham, and Mahon learned it nearly as easily as the rest of us.'

'Well, that's the solution, then,' said Aidan lightly. 'If Gabur were gone, your father would probably appoint Owen as his assistant; Owen's twenty-one now, he'll soon be a qualified lawyer. You shouldn't have stopped Mahon hitting Gabur with that stone, Diarmuid. That's the only way out for him. He has to kill off Gabur.'

Chapter Two 🍀

Supper was over, and still there was no sign of Mahon. Gabur hadn't appeared either, but that wasn't surprising. Everyone knew that he was soon to be married. Nessa, his bride-to-be, was only a year older than Ita, and she wasn't very keen on Gabur — everyone knew that as well. She wanted to marry a young horn player called Finbar; but her father, Dara, had insisted on the match with Gabur, and the wedding was to be soon. Gabur often took his evening meal with Nessa and Dara in their house at Drummoher, only a couple of miles from Drumshee.

'Great to be without Gabur, isn't it?' said Cathal, jumping over a stool and swinging from the crossbeam of the little kitchen-house where they had all their meals. 'It's a shame it's too late for a game of hurley.'

Old Fionnuala had gone back to her own house, leaving Owen in charge. Owen, however, was too busy studying for his final examinations to take much notice of the younger students. He sat by the fire, his fingers in his ears and his lips busily moving.

'Maybe he'll stay out all night,' said Aidan gleefully, catching hold of Cathal's legs and trying to swing from them.

'You'll bring the house down,' observed Diarmuid. 'I swear I saw the thatch shake there.'

'Pull your legs up, Aidan,' shouted Cathal. 'Now hold on tight and I'll give you a swing.'

With a shout of glee, Aidan drew up his legs; Cathal bent down until his red head almost touched Aidan's black one, and they swung together. Then, with a gust of wind that blew the smoke from the fire, the door was flung open.

Instantly all was silent. Even Owen felt the change in the air; he took his fingers from his ears and looked around in a bewildered way. Cathal and Aidan landed with a thud on the floor and stood there guiltily, staring at the door. Only Gabur would burst through a door like that.

After a moment, an undersized, sandy-haired boy slid around the door, a smirk on his pale, freckled face.

'I scared you,' he said triumphantly.

'It's only Ciarán,' said Fergal with disdain. 'It's the physician's brat of an apprentice. Go away, Ciarán. No one has a cough or the sniffles here. We don't need you.'

'I was sent with a message to Fionnuala,' replied Ciarán, sidling into the room, his pale, boiled-gooseberry eyes flickering over everyone.

'Tell us and we'll tell her,' commanded Diarmuid.

For a moment Ciarán seemed inclined to argue, but they all closed in around him and he thought better of it.

'My master, Colm the physician, told me to tell Fionnuala that his brother, Gabur the lawyer, will not be back at Drumshee until quite late tonight,' he recited, in the tone of someone who has learnt a lesson off by heart.

'Oh, brilliant!' said Aidan.

'Where's he gone, then?' asked Cathal.

'My master didn't tell me,' said Ciarán nervously. 'Gabur came to see him, and I heard them shouting. I think they had a quarrel. Then Brendan the cattle-dealer came, and Gabur went away with Brendan.'

'Is that Brendan from over Kinvarra way?' Owen asked. 'A big fellow, big and fat?'

Ciarán nodded. Owen gave a long, low whistle.

'He won't stay long with him,' said Diarmuid wisely. 'Brendan hates him. He was one of Gabur's clients; I'm not sure what happened, but Brendan lost a lot of money because of something Gabur did. I heard the brehon getting very angry with Gabur about that. Where were they going, Ciarán?'

Ciarán said, 'I think they were going towards the little house near the bog-land, beyond the Isle of Maain. You know, where Eithne lives. Yesterday I heard Brendan telling Eithne that he was going to bring Gabur down to talk to her.'

'Well...!' said Cathal. The boys all looked at one another with knowing smirks on their faces.

Ita was puzzled. There was some secret about Gabur and Eithne. She had noticed the boys doing that before, when their names came up. She would ask Fionnuala, she decided.

'I wouldn't think he'd be likely to go there,' said Diarmuid thoughtfully. 'Or at least, if he did, he wouldn't stay all the evening.'

'More likely he's gone off to Drummoher to see Nessa,' said Aidan, kissing the air in a way that made them all laugh — except Diarmuid, who blushed furiously. He was in love with the beautiful red-haired Nessa.

'We're going to have a great evening,' said Fergal, his black eyes sparkling and his dark-skinned face full of excitement. 'It's a pity poor old Mahon isn't here. Someone should go and look for him. Cathal and I will go. We'll keep shouting for him. He might come back if he knows that swine Gabur isn't going to be about for a few hours.'

'I like Gabur,' said Ciarán smugly. 'He gave me a piece of silver.'

'What!' Aidan stared at him, open-mouthed. 'What on earth did he do that for?'

'He said I was a clever boy, and he gave me the silver. He said he'd never met such a clever boy. And then he went off to talk to Colm.'

Everyone stared at him in disbelief.

'You couldn't be cleverer than Ninian,' Diarmuid said eventually. 'He has only to hear something once and he remembers it for ever. Does anyone remember ever hearing Gabur say that Ninian was clever?'

'Never,' chorused all the law students. Even Owen was listening with interest.

'And does anyone remember Gabur ever giving Ninian a piece of silver?' continued Diarmuid.

'Never!' repeated everyone.

'You're a liar, Ciarán,' said Aidan.

'No, I'm not,' said Ciarán indignantly, opening his pouch. 'Look, you can see for yourselves. There's the piece of silver.'

Everyone gazed at it. It was definitely a piece of silver.

'Well, you'd better tell us that wonderful thing you did that made Gabur give you a piece of silver,' said Fergal sarcastically.

'Well, he wanted something for a headache, and I told him feverfew was the right stuff for that, and he looked at my foxglove seeds and asked whether those would do, and I told him that too many fox-glove seeds can kill a man,' said Ciarán proudly. 'And then he smiled and gave me the piece of silver, and then he went in to see Colm.'

There was a silence. Everyone stared at Ciarán in a puzzled way. Why on earth would Gabur find fever-few and foxglove seeds so interesting?

'We're wasting our evening,' said Ita. 'Fergal, you and Cathal go and see if you can find Mahon. I'll go and give Fionnuala the message from Gabur, and I'll see if she'll give us some honey-cakes so we can have a party.'

'And I'll just hang Ciarán by his feet from the crossbeam,' said Aidan, his brown eyes glinting with fun. 'Maybe some of his brains will leak out on me, and then Gabur will give me some silver tomorrow.'

Ciarán didn't wait; he was out of the door in a flash. Ita laughed and followed him out.

The law school was built inside the ancient walls of the Drumshee fort. There were five buildings there: the schoolhouse; the scholars' house, where the students and Fionnuala and her deaf old husband Donogh lived; the kitchen-house, where they ate the meals that Fionnuala cooked; Gabur's house; and the brehon's house, where Ita and her father lived. Ita's mother had died when Ita was only four years old, and Flann the brehon had kept his little daughter with him, not allowing her to be fostered by another family as the custom was. He hadn't wanted to be parted from her. As Ita grew older, she had joined in the work at the law school, and Flann was very proud of her cleverness.

'You won't be the first woman brehon, though,' he had told her. 'I've never met one myself, but there is something in the judgement texts about a female judge.'

Well, if I'm ever in charge of the law school, I'll make sure that I don't have someone like Gabur bullying the students, thought Ita as she crossed the yard towards the scholars' house.

'Fionnuala,' she said, as she went into the house, 'Gabur has sent a message to say that he'll be late back this evening.'

Fionnuala rose up from the fire, her small round face filled with pleasure.

'Well, praise to the sun god,' she said. 'I wouldn't mind doing without him for ever. How's that poor boy Mahon?'

'Oh, he ran away and hid, but Cathal and Fergal have gone to look for him. They'll find him.... And, Fionnuala, could we have a few honey-cakes, if you can spare them? We thought we'd have a little party.'

Fionnuala beamed. Ita was like her own child; she had looked after her for most of her life, and she loved her more than anyone else in the world.

'You can indeed. It isn't often that you all have a bit of fun. I'll give you something nice to drink, too. It's got some mead in it,' she added, lowering her voice to a whisper.

Ita smiled with pleasure. Mead was strong stuff; it was made by fermenting honey, and you didn't need much to make you feel very merry indeed.

'Where's Gabur, then?' asked Fionnuala, bustling around the little house.

'Ciarán thought he went towards Eithne's house,' said Ita.

Fionnuala stopped, her mouth open in surprise. 'Never!' she said.

There it is again, thought Ita. There's definitely a mystery here.

She put an arm around the old woman's shoulders; Ita was small for her age, but Fionnuala was tiny, and already Ita was a few inches taller.

'Fionnuala,' she said coaxingly, 'tell me about Gabur and Eithne. What happened?'

Fionnuala looked at her doubtfully. She loved to gossip; Ita knew that the old woman was only looking for an excuse to tell her everything.

'Oh, go on, Fionnuala, tell me. After all, I'm thirteen now. I could be married soon.'

'I don't know what your father would say if he knew you'd been listening to these old stories,' said Fionnuala, obviously weakening.

'Oh, he wouldn't take any notice,' said Ita scornfully. 'He never notices anything that isn't to do with the law.'

'Well, in a way, this is to do with the law,' said Fionnuala. 'You know the Brehon Law says that if a man has a child by a woman who he isn't married to, he can acknowledge this child as his own, and the child can inherit the man's property?'

Ita nodded. This was one of the thousands of laws that she had been memorising from an early age.

'Well,' continued Fionnuala, 'when Gabur was a young man, he and Eithne lived together as man and wife, but they never married. And when Eithne had a son — that's young Lorcan — Gabur left her and said the baby wasn't his. Lorcan must be fourteen or fifteen now. He *is* Gabur's son; you only have to look at the two of them to see how alike they are — they've both got those big heads and sticking-out teeth. But Gabur has never acknowledged him; and

Eithne and Lorcan are as poor as can be, and Gabur does nothing for them. They both hate Gabur as much as any living creature can hate another.'

'I think everyone hates Gabur,' said Ita, taking the basket of honey-cakes and the flask of mead. 'All of us do, anyway.'

'So do I,' whispered Fionnuala. 'Do you know what he's up to now? He's trying to make your father turn me and Donogh out of this house. He says Donogh is no good for work, now that he's so deaf. I keep hoping that, one dark night, Gabur will fall into the River Fergus and get himself drowned. There won't be many would miss him, I can tell you that.'

'I'll talk to my father,' promised Ita, quite shocked. She couldn't imagine doing without Fionnuala to mother her and spoil her. 'I'm going to talk to him about Mahon, too. Gabur is ruining his life.'

'So he is — and he's doing his best to ruin Donogh's life, too,' said Fionnuala bitterly. 'He talked to Donogh this evening before he went out — shouting at him, he was. Donogh knew what he was saying, and he was so upset that he took himself off out of the house without a word. He's been gone for two hours now, and that's not like him.'

'The world would be a better place without Gabur,' said Ita thoughtfully.

'So it would,' agreed Fionnuala. 'No one would waste a tear if he were found dead.'

Chapter Three 🌸

'**H**e's dead,' screamed Mahon, bursting through the door of the little house. His face was as white as his linen tunic, and his rough dark hair was standing on end.

There was an instant silence.

Fergal and Cathal had arrived back over an hour before, and although Mahon was nowhere to be found, the other six had managed to enjoy themselves immensely. The house had filled with excited voices, laughter, snatches of song. Old Fionnuala had come over to enjoy the fun; she sat by the fireplace, smiling happily at the students.

Now there was no smile on anyone's face. Everyone just stood there, as if suddenly turned into stone, and each face turned the same white as Mahon's. They stared at him incredulously.

'Who's dead?' asked Ita eventually; but she knew the answer to her own question.

'Gabur,' whispered Mahon.

The other students took a step back, staring at him in horror. Fionnuala put her hands across her mouth. Mahon held on to the still-open door, unable to say anything else. He looked as if he would fall down in a dead faint at any moment.

Owen got up from his seat by the fire and crossed the room. He took Mahon's hand from the door and, with an arm around the shaking boy, steered him across the floor and pushed him into the fireside seat.

'Give me some mead for him, Fionnuala,' he said quietly.

Fionnuala seemed unable to stir. Ita, doing her best to keep her hand steady, poured mead into a wooden goblet and held it to Mahon's lips. He sipped, and then drank thirstily. Ita took a honey-cake from the basket, broke off a bit and fed him as if he were a starving bird. It was easier than saying anything — easier than asking him questions. The other five boys came a step closer, still staring at him with pale faces.

It's funny, thought Ita: so often, we've all wished that Gabur was dead. And now he is dead, and it's the most terrible thing. I wish my father were here. I wonder if Owen knows what to do....

The same question had obviously occurred to Owen. He was nervously twisting his fingers and looking around him. Mahon sat with his head in his hands, but the other boys had gathered around and were staring at him.

Owen squared his shoulders and took a deep breath.

'Diarmuid,' he said quietly, 'will you go and fetch Colm the physician? He needs to know. Gabur is his brother, and ... and maybe Mahon is wrong. Maybe Gabur isn't really dead. Maybe he's just unconscious.'

Mahon raised his head. A little colour had come back into his cheeks, Ita noticed.

'I'm not stupid,' he said harshly. 'I know a dead man when I see one. The back of his head has been completely smashed in by a big stone. He's dead all right.'

A shiver of horror went through the others. Ita

took her hand off Mahon's arm and then put it back again. Whatever he had done, he needed comfort just now.

Owen jerked his head at Diarmuid, and Diarmuid, with one backward glance at Mahon, slid out of the door. The others looked at one another, at the fire, or at the roof; but no one looked at Mahon. The picture of Gabur lying on the ground with his head broken by a stone was vivid in all of their minds.

Owen took a deep breath. The question had to be asked, and it was up to him, as the eldest, to ask it.

'What happened, Mahon?' he asked.

Mahon shook his head in a bewildered way. 'I d-d-don't know,' he said, and his tongue stumbled over the three simple words.

Fionnuala got up from her seat by the fire and went to Owen.

'Now, Owen,' she whispered authoritatively, 'there's no need to make too much of all this. There's no one but ourselves need know anything about it. We can all say that Mahon was here with us for the whole evening, and then he and Aidan went out, and they found Gabur and came back here to tell us all. You'll say that, Aidan, won't you?'

Aidan nodded. There was no trace of the usual fun in his face. He looked strained and anxious.

'Then run after Diarmuid and tell him to tell Colm the same story,' said Fionnuala.

We can't do that, thought Ita. Even as the thought crossed her mind, Owen put out a hand and held Aidan back.

'No,' he said decisively. 'We're lawyers — law students, anyway. We're supposed to look for the truth. We can't do this. We can't start telling lies.'

'Lies!' said Fionnuala, her face going a bright red. 'What's lies next to ruining a boy's life for ever? The lad is only fourteen years old. Do you want that hanging over him for the rest of his life? That father of his will never let him forget it. He'll have to pay Gabur's honour-price to Colm, and it will ruin him.'

Ita tilted the goblet towards Mahon's lips and he gulped down some more mead. He was beginning to look more normal.

'I'm telling you, Owen,' continued Fionnuala indignantly, 'you'll live to regret this day. Why ruin a boy's life for the sake of someone like Gabur? Aren't we all better off without him? Let Aidan go after Diarmuid while you think about it. It'll only delay Colm a few minutes, and Mahon is sure that Gabur is dead, anyway.'

Owen hesitated, and the others held their breath. Then Owen nodded at Aidan, and Aidan shot off. He was the best runner in the school; he would easily catch Diarmuid.

Ita let out her breath in a great sigh of relief. Maybe Fionnuala was right, after all; maybe this night would be something that they would all bury at the bottoms of their minds and never think of again.

She looked around. Owen looked very troubled. Ita felt sorry for him: he had a terrible decision in front of him, and he knew what Flann the brehon, her father, would say. Cathal was nervously tugging a lock of his red hair. Ninian's narrow, clever face looked as troubled as Owen's. He was another born lawyer; the truth would be everything to him. Fergal's small dark face was serious and concentrated. He went over and knelt on the floor beside Mahon, the firelight glinting on his smooth black hair.

'Mahon,' he asked quietly, 'where did you find Gabur?'

'Beside the River Fergus, just where it goes down underground, before you come to Ballycasheen — at the Clab.'

Fergal waited a moment and then said, quite casually, 'Did you kill him?'

Waves of shock went through the room. No one really wanted to hear the answer.

There was a moment of silence; then Mahon's dull eyes widened and he looked straight at Fergal.

'No,' he said in a tired voice. 'No, of course I didn't.'

Ita desperately wanted to believe him, but as she looked around she could see her own doubts in the others' eyes. Perhaps it was the tiredness in Mahon's voice, but he didn't sound very sure; he didn't even sound indignant.

Fionnuala cleared her throat. The door opened and Diarmuid and Aidan came back in. Aidan was sweating, but Diarmuid looked quite cool: his blond hair was still neatly combed back from his high forehead, and his tanned face was its normal colour. He obviously wasn't hurrying on the way to Colm's house, thought Ita. It was also obvious that Aidan had told him about Fionnuala's suggestion. They both stood in the centre of the room, looking awkward and embarrassed.

Owen glanced at Mahon worriedly. Poor Owen, thought Ita. It's very bad luck on him that Father isn't here.

She looked at Mahon. She had known him since she was five years old — longer than she had known any of the others. As young children they had played together. He had always been very good to her, very gentle, very kind. In fact, she thought, as the shock began to ebb out of her mind, Mahon's always been gentle and kind to everything — farmyard animals, kittens, even the hares in the field. He hates to see anything suffer.

Suddenly she knelt beside him, put her hand on his rough hair and twisted his head around so that she could look into his eyes.

'Mahon,' she said softly, 'tell us the truth. Did you kill Gabur?'

Mahon shuddered, and for an instant a cold feeling came over Ita. Was he going to say he had done it?

Then the shuddering stopped; Mahon looked directly at Ita and said, quite simply, 'No, Ita, I didn't.'

This time his voice carried conviction.

Ita stood up. 'Send for Colm, Owen,' she said clearly. 'We'll have to tell him that Mahon found Gabur's body and no one knows who murdered him.'

'Just tell him to come, Diarmuid,' said Owen, looking relieved that the decision had been taken out of his hands. 'Tell him that there's been a bad accident and we need him urgently. Bring him straight here.'

Ita unhooked a couple of the cloaks that hung on the back of the door. She put them around Mahon and tucked him in. These cloaks were made from three layers of wool, and were so warm that Mahon would probably sleep under them. At least they would stop his shivering before he had to face the questions from Gabur's brother, Colm the physician.

Chapter Four

A full hour had passed by the candle clock, and still there was no sign of Diarmuid or of Colm. The other boys went off to the scholars' house and left Fionnuala, Ita and Owen all staring at the peacefully sleeping Mahon. Old Donogh came in and sat down sleepily on the seat on the other side of the fire. Fionnuala gave him an anxious glance, but he didn't look at her.

Owen got to his feet. 'I'm going out,' he said. 'I must make sure that Gabur is dead. I know the place. It's the Clab, isn't it? I'll take a pony and go straight to Ballycasheen.'

He was gone in an instant.

'He's glad to have something to do,' said Ita in a whisper to Fionnuala. 'He doesn't want to stand around looking at Mahon and wondering if he did it.'

'Shh,' said Fionnuala, but Mahon hadn't stirred. He seemed fast asleep under the warmth of the cloaks.

'It's a shame,' continued Fionnuala. 'But I suppose that sooner or later someone would have talked.'

'We have to know the truth,' said Ita stubbornly. 'Mahon can't go through his life with everyone wondering whether he murdered a man or not.'

Fionnuala said no more, but her face was disapproving. Ita pushed uncomfortable thoughts to the back of her head and went to the door.

It was quite dark already, she noticed when she opened it. The days were getting shorter and shorter; soon it would be Midwinter Day. The moon showed silver in the south-eastern sky, and Venus shone brightly nearby.

She thought she heard something, and she strained her ears. It seemed to be the noise of a pony stumbling over the rough stones of the lane below. Probably Colm, she thought. Owen wouldn't ride so slowly. Colm must have given Diarmuid a ride back.

She saw the wavering light of a little lantern; the small flame of the candle, flickering inside the lantern's sheltering transparent sheets of horn, steadied, and the noise of the pony's footsteps ceased. Colm's letting Diarmuid get down, Ita thought. The double weight up the steep hill to Drumshee would be too much for the pony.

'They're here,' she said quietly to Fionnuala. 'I'll just run down and meet them.'

'Take your cloak,' said Fionnuala, but Ita was gone. She had to see Diarmuid before she talked to Colm.

Quickly she ran across the Togher Field. Colm would ride up the pathway; Diarmuid would take the short cut through the field.

'What did he say?' she hissed as soon as Diarmuid's lanky form came into view.

'Well, I told him there'd been an accident,' said Diarmuid, 'and, of course, he wanted to know who was hurt. I had to tell him that it was Gabur, even though Owen told me not to say. It would've been stupid to pretend that I didn't know.'

'How did he take it?' asked Ita curiously.

'He just said, straight out, "Is he still alive?" and I said I didn't know. Then he packed his bag and told me to jump on to the pony behind him, and we came over as quickly as we could.'

'You took ages,' said Ita over her shoulder, running ahead of him up the steep, waterlogged field.

'He was sleeping when I got there,' explained Diarmuid, panting along behind her. 'I had to wait for him to get dressed.'

They barely reached the gate of the enclosure before Colm came in. It's a good thing he was going so slowly, thought Ita. Diarmuid's skinny, but even so, his weight and Colm's must have tired out the pony.

She dashed across the enclosure and in the door of the kitchen-house. The other boys had disappeared, but Mahon was still sleeping, and Fionnuala was still standing there with that frozen look of fear on her face. Old Donogh still dozed peacefully beside the fire.

'Where's Gabur?' was Colm's first question as he came in.

'At the Clab, near Ballycasheen,' said Fionnuala.

'I should have gone straight there,' said Colm, turning to go out. 'Is anyone with him?'

'Owen has gone,' said Ita.

'Who found him?' asked Colm, his voice loud enough to rouse Donogh. The old man sat up with a start, dropping the iron poker that he had been holding in his hand.

The crash roused Mahon. He sat up, bewildered and still sleepy. He looked at Colm, and the horror of the last few hours was still in his eyes. Ita crossed the room swiftly, but it was too late. Still half-asleep, Mahon blurted out, 'Colm, Gabur's dead. The back of his head has been smashed in. Everyone thinks I did it.'

Colm was a nice man; they had always said that,

all of them. No one at the law school could understand how such a nice man could have such a foul
and horrible brother. Colm crossed the room and
knelt beside Mahon's stool. There was no trace of
anger in his face; just compassion and sympathy.

'What happened, Mahon?' he asked.

'I was hiding.... Gabur — Gabur came along,' said
Mahon jerkily. He stopped and swallowed, and then
went on. 'I saw him fall down.... I ran — I think I
ran.... There was blood all over — on his head — all
the bone was smashed —' Mahon stopped again and
clapped both hands over his mouth. His stomach
was heaving. Fionnuala ran to get a basin, but after a
minute Mahon took his hands away and leaned his
head back against the wall. His face was a dirty
shade of yellow.

'He won't be sick; I don't suppose he's had anything to eat since breakfast,' said Ita. 'He was too
upset after ...' She stopped, remembering what had
upset Mahon. She must warn all the boys not to
mention the savage beating that Gabur had given
Mahon that morning.

Colm, however, wasn't taking much notice of
either of them. He was touching Mahon's clammy
skin with a concerned hand and putting a finger over
the veins on his wrist.

'Drink this,' he said, pouring out some red liquid
from a small flask in his bag and holding it to
Mahon's lips. 'Get him to bed, Fionnuala. He's had a
bad shock. I've given him something to help him
sleep. There's no point in him dozing on the stool;
he'll fall in the fire if you leave him there. Here, I'll
give you a hand with him. Ita, you take the lamp.'

The other boys were in the scholars' house, lying

on their beds, talking in subdued voices. They jumped to their feet, their faces white and scared, when they saw the drooping figure of Mahon in Colm's grip.

'Go and sit in the kitchen, boys,' Colm said quietly. 'Mahon needs to sleep now. No one is to disturb him until I come back. Is there a key to this door?' he added, looking at Fionnuala.

Fionnuala took it from the bunch she wore at her waist and handed it to him. She looked tired and worried, and older than Ita had ever seen her.

Colm put the bedcovers over Mahon and then turned away, ushering the others out in front of him. Mahon already seemed to have dropped back into sleep. His black eyelashes were flat against his cheeks, and his breaths sounded deep and slow.

'He'll be all right now,' said Colm, locking the door and putting the key in his pocket. 'Ita, will you get Donogh to come with me on his own pony? We can bring Gabur's body back, slung between the two ponies. I've brought a leather stretcher with me.'

'He must believe that Gabur is dead,' said Fergal, when Colm and Donogh had gone trotting down the pathway.

Ninian nodded. 'Well, if he believed Mahon, he must know that. A man can't survive a smashed skull like that.'

'Do you remember what we were talking about this morning?' asked Aidan. 'Remember, I said that Gabur beat Mahon for not knowing what the fine is for a secret killing? It seems funny now....'

His voice trailed away. The others were looking at him in horror.

'Funny!' said Ita.

'Shut up, Aidan,' said Cathal, his ears going as red as his hair.

'I don't mean funny, exactly,' said Aidan quickly. 'I mean strange. I didn't mean *funny*, honestly I didn't. I think it's dreadful. After all, Gabur's dead — and if Mahon did it, he'll have to pay for it. It's just that ... that now we do have a secret killing here at Drumshee. What is the fine for it, anyway?'

Cathal shrugged. 'Well, the fine for a killing is twenty-one ounces of silver, or twenty-one cows. Mahon couldn't pay that. His father would have to pay it.'

'That's impossible,' said Fergal. 'His father can't have much more than twenty cows. How will he and the others live if he has to pay that for Mahon's fine?'

'It's more than that,' said Cathal, with horror. 'I've just remembered. That's not all. That's just the fine. What's the honour-price for a brehon?'

'Five ounces of silver,' said Diarmuid.

'No, it would only be three ounces for Gabur,' argued Ita. 'My father's worth five ounces, but Gabur is only worth three, because he's a brehon of the lowest degree. But still, that makes twenty-four ounces of silver, or twenty-four cows.'

'Wait a minute,' said Ninian. 'Unless Mahon says that he did it and why he did it, then it will be counted as a secret killing. You know what the fine for a secret killing is, don't you?'

'No, we don't,' said Cathal impatiently. 'Go on, Ninian, you tell us. You always remember everything.'

'The fine for a secret and unlawful killing,' said Ninian, slowly and impressively, 'is twice the normal fine for murder. So the fine for Gabur's killing would be forty-two ounces of silver; and to that you must add the honour-price of three ounces of silver. That means that Mahon's father and the kin-group, if necessary, would have to pay forty-five ounces of silver, or forty-five cows.'

Everyone gasped, but no one had time to say anything. The door had opened and in walked a middle-aged man with a grey beard, wearing a lawyer's gown.

'It's good to hear you all learning the laws so well,' said Flann.

'Father!' said Ita. Then she stopped. It was impossible to explain. She felt like bursting into tears. She looked at Ninian, but he avoided her eye.

She took a deep breath, but Fergal stepped forward. He fixed his dark eyes on Flann's face and spoke clearly.

'Master,' he said with a low bow. 'Welcome back. I hope your business with the King went well.'

'Very well,' said Flann, looking amused. 'It's gone very well. And I have great news for you all. King Carthen is coming to attend the midwinter celebrations at Coad in seven days' time. You will all be able to see him there.'

No one moved or smiled or exclaimed. He looked at them with puzzlement.

'Where's Owen?' he asked, looking around the room.

'He's gone out. He's with Colm the physician. There's been an accident. We think Gabur is dead.'

'Dead!' said Flann, with a sharp note of alarm in his voice. 'What happened? Has he been killed? Did someone kill him?'

✿ Chapter Five

Why had he said that? The question kept going through Ita's mind. Why had her father assumed that it was murder? Why not an accident, a fatal illness?

Whatever the reason for the question, it opened the floodgates.

'We thought it might have been Mahon,' blurted out Aidan.

'Stupid,' said Cathal furiously.

'Why?' enquired Flann.

'Because he is stupid,' muttered Cathal. 'Aidan, I mean,' he added.

'No, I mean why did you think it might be Mahon? And where is Mahon?'

'In bed,' said Ita. 'Colm gave him some medicine. He's asleep.'

'And why did you think that he killed Gabur?' repeated Flann.

There was silence for a moment.

'Ninian?' said Flann, fixing him with a severe look.

'You see, sir,' said Ninian earnestly, 'we thought Mahon had done it because Gabur beat him so badly this morning, and Mahon said that he would ...' His voice trailed away, and he gave a guilty look at Ita.

Now why did he have to say that? thought Ita. I suppose he's just used to giving all the right answers in class.

Chapter Five

'What did Mahon say he would do?' enquired Flann.

Ninian gave a despairing look around, but all the others had their eyes on the floor.

'He said he would kill Gabur,' Ninian muttered eventually.

'But he didn't,' said Fergal hastily.

Flann took no notice of him. His eyes were fixed intently on Ninian.

'Who found the body?' he asked.

'Mahon,' said Ninian reluctantly.

'Anyone with him?'

Ninian shook his head miserably.

'How long had Mahon been missing?'

No one answered.

'One hour? Two hours?'

'All afternoon,' said Ninian eventually.

'I see,' said Flann thoughtfully.

'Mahon didn't do it, Father,' said Ita, trying to make her voice carry as much conviction as possible.

'Oh,' said her father. 'Why do you think that? Do you know what happened? Do you know who killed Gabur?'

'No,' muttered Ita. Fionnuala got up and put an arm around her. Ita felt that she would love to sit on Fionnuala's lap, as she had when she was younger, but she had to do her best for Mahon.

'Mahon said he didn't do it,' she continued bravely. 'Fergal asked him, and I asked him again. He said he didn't do it.'

'They're coming back,' interrupted Diarmuid, crossing the floor and opening the door.

No one went to the door with him. They all hung back, dreading what they were going to see. Flann moved forward and put Diarmuid behind him.

Ita sat down on the stool by the fire and held her hands out to the smouldering pieces of turf. She felt weak and cold, almost as if she were ill. She could hear her father talking in a low voice to Colm, but she couldn't hear the words.

Then they heard the noise of the pony's feet moving over the roughly paved ground of the fort. Owen came in, looking white and young.

'Is he dead?' asked Diarmuid.

Owen nodded.

'Where was he?' asked Aidan.

'Just by the big cliff at the Clab, near where the River Fergus goes underground. He was lying on his face, and the back of his head was completely smashed. There was a big stone beside him, covered in blood.'

Ita shuddered.

'It must have been an accident,' said Fionnuala resolutely. 'He was walking along and a stone fell out of the cliff and hit him on the head.'

Owen shook his head. He looked dead tired. 'Then it would have been the top of his head. The stone hit him on the back of the head, just above his neck.'

'Perhaps he was looking down, or even lying down,' muttered Fionnuala, but even she didn't sound too convinced.

No one else said anything. They were all silently looking at one another when Flann and Colm came in.

Ita studied her father's face, but there was nothing to be read there. Colm looked upset, though not grief-stricken — more uncomfortable, really, Ita decided; almost as if he didn't know what to do.

'He's only a boy,' he was saying in a low voice. 'Gabur could be very cruel, you know.'

Chapter Five

'Let's go out,' whispered Ita to the others. The six of them, followed by Fionnuala and Donogh, filed silently out through the door.

Aidan shut the door carefully; then, when Donogh and Fionnuala had gone back to their own room in the scholars' house, he quickly put his ear to the wide crack between the door and the wall of the kitchen-house.

'Aidan!' whispered Owen. 'Come away at once.'

'No,' whispered Ita. 'We've got to know what's happening. We've got to be able to help Mahon.'

Without hesitation, she moved up beside Aidan. The others crowded around. They could all hear, although the two men inside spoke in low tones.

'I won't push the matter,' Colm was saying. 'I know I have a right to the blood-price, but surely I also have the right not to claim it. Gabur has no close kin-folk, other than me. I make no claim against the boy.'

'That's if he did it,' said Flann mildly. 'Did he? Are you sure?'

There was a moment's silence, and then Colm's voice came again, stumbling slightly: 'He must have. Who else?'

'Who indeed?' said Flann thoughtfully. 'He was not greatly loved, your brother. You said it yourself. He could be cruel.'

That's right, thought Ita. Everyone hated him. It might not have been Mahon. She and Aidan looked at each other; and then they nearly fell forwards into the kitchen-house as the door was suddenly opened.

'What are you doing there?' enquired Flann sternly.

'Just going to study,' muttered Aidan.

'We can't go into our room,' said Fergal quickly. 'Mahon's in there and Colm has locked the door.'

'You could go to the schoolhouse, if you really want to study,' said Colm, with an attempt at a smile.

'No, wait,' said Flann. 'Let them come with us. They're all Mahon's friends. Let them be with him while we see what he has to say. I think the boy might prefer that to having his father here.'

That means we must be on Mahon's side: we are his lawyers, thought Ita, feeling slightly comforted. Her father was a judge, and he had often told them that a judge must hear both sides of a story before he even starts to make up his mind. He wouldn't make up his mind until he had heard what Mahon had to say.

'Give me a minute with him before you come in,' said Colm, taking the key from his pocket. 'He may be still drowsy. It's not fair to talk to him while he's half-asleep. I'll call you.'

Only a few minutes passed before Colm came back out again and beckoned to them. When they went in, Mahon was sitting on the side of his bed, his face still flushed with sleep, but his eyes wide open and alert. Ita noticed that his rough brown hair was slightly damp around the forehead; obviously Colm had sponged his face to wake him up.

She perched on the bed beside him. The others crowded together on Fergal's bed, which was beside Mahon's. Flann and Colm sat on stools.

'Tell us exactly what happened, Mahon; leave nothing out,' said Flann.

'I was out near Ballycasheen, just near where the River Fergus goes underground,' began Mahon. 'I saw Gabur walking along. He didn't see me.'

'Why not? Were you hiding?' asked Flann.

Chapter Five

Mahon nodded.

'Where?'

Mahon hesitated. 'In the bushes,' he said eventually.

That's a lie, thought Ita. She looked at Fergal and saw a worried frown appear between his dark eyes. He was thinking the same thing she was: it was stupid of Mahon to start off by lying to Flann. The brehon always spotted a lie instantly.

However, Flann said nothing; he just waited blandly for Mahon to continue.

'Gabur was ... was quite near me when he ... he fell,' said Mahon, stumbling over his words. Ita squeezed his hand encouragingly, and after a moment he returned the pressure. Flann and Colm waited patiently, Colm's face concerned and gentle, Flann's a blank mask.

'I didn't see what had happened, but I heard a noise ... just as he fell — a sort ... a sort of bang, like a stone hitting a rock. I waited for a while, I waited for him to get up. I thought he had tripped and fallen. Then, when he didn't get up, I came out and went over to him. His face was on the ground and the back of his head was smashed in.'

'Did you throw a stone at him?' enquired Flann.

Mahon shook his head.

'It would be hard for a lad of that age to throw a heavy stone with such force that it crushed a man's skull,' remarked Colm.

Mahon looked up. For the first time there was some hope in his face.

'Hand me your pouch,' said Flann quietly.

Mahon took his hand from Ita's and silently handed over the pouch that he wore around his waist. Flann walked over to Diarmuid's bed and opened it.

'One knife,' he said, placing it on the bed. 'One piece of linen, badly in need of washing; one snare made from wire; one small stone —'

'I gave him that,' interrupted Ita. 'It's a lucky stone.'

'One apple,' continued Flann, ignoring his daughter and placing the stone next to the snare. 'One plain cloak-pin, badly bent; one sling.'

He laid the sling on the bed beside the other things. Although his voice had not changed, the atmosphere had. Everyone stared at the sling. What was it that Aidan said this morning? thought Ita. *'Why don't you sling a stone at him? You'll easily hit him; you're great with your sling.'* Aidan's words rang in her head, and she knew that the other boys were thinking of them as well.

'Why did you have a sling with you, Mahon?' asked Flann.

Mahon looked at him in a bewildered way.

Ita jumped to her feet. 'That's not fair, Father,' she said. 'All the boys carry their slings in their pouches. Go on, Fergal, show him — go on, all of you; open your pouches.'

Hastily they fumbled in their pouches, while Ita sent up a fervent prayer to the sun god that none of them had tidied their pouches recently. Her prayers were answered: each pouch contained a jumble of objects, and each one of them had a leather sling.

'Well done, Ita,' said her father. 'You've proved your point. The sling is not evidence.' He had a half-smile on his face, but it vanished when he turned back to Mahon.

'Mahon,' he said, 'you know enough of the law to know that the killing of a man in hot temper, if it is admitted afterwards, is not as serious as a secret killing. I am asking you now, if you did kill Gabur, to tell me, and I will do my best for you.'

Mahon shook his head firmly. He looked straight into Flann's eyes and said, 'I didn't kill him.'

Colm got up from the stool and came across to the bed. Gently he moved Ita aside, sat down beside Mahon and put an arm around him.

'Mahon,' he said earnestly, 'if you admit to killing Gabur, that will be the end of the matter. I won't ask for any blood-money. I've heard from Ciarán how you were treated, and I was ashamed of my brother. You'll owe me nothing, but we must know the truth.'

Flann moved uneasily. 'Some sort of recompense must be paid,' he said. 'Murder can't be ignored.'

'Then he can pay it off with labour,' said Colm. 'He can come and work in my herb garden for the next six months. I need to grow herbs to make my medicines, but Ciarán isn't very good at digging. Mahon is strong for his age; I've seen the way he helps Donogh with your vegetable garden. He can work for me. That will be the blood-price for my brother's death.'

Ita looked around. Her father's face was hard to read, but the faces of the five boys on the other bed were well-known to her. A sort of incredulous joy was spreading amongst them. This was a better outcome than anyone could have dared to hope for. Soon Aidan will be turning somersaults, she thought.

She gazed thoughtfully at the boy beside her and realised that Mahon wouldn't go along with a lie. Suddenly she was glad of it.

She held her head high and gazed fiercely at her father.

'The law is there to find the truth,' she said to him.

It was his favourite phrase, and every one of his students knew it by heart.

He gave her a half-smile, but his eyes immediately returned to Mahon's face.

Mahon met his eyes with no hesitation.

'No,' he said. 'No. I didn't kill him.'

And that was the end of the evening. Flann sent all the boys, including Owen, to bed, and stayed in the scholars' house for some time to make sure that there was no trouble. Fionnuala came across to the brehon's house with Ita and stayed with her until she heard Flann and Colm come in.

'You go to sleep now, Ita,' she said, rising to her feet. 'I'll make the two of them some hot mead and then I'll be off back to Donogh.'

'Fionnuala,' said Ita, sitting up in bed, 'tell my father to come and see me. I want to talk to him. Tell him I'm not asleep.'

A few minutes later, Flann came in and sat silently on the side of her bed.

'What will happen now?' she asked.

'Well, tomorrow we'll bury Gabur,' he said simply.

Ita shuddered. 'Not here, Father,' she said earnestly, 'not here, not where Mother's buried. I don't want him here outside our fort.'

'No,' said her father calmly. 'He'll be buried outside Colm's fort at Caherblonick. That's the right place for him. I've sent Donogh to tell Finbar, the horn player; he'll play the lament.'

'Finbar won't lament Gabur; he'll be pleased,' Ita said thoughtfully. 'Now he might be able to marry Nessa. Her father wouldn't let her because a horn player is of low status compared to a lawyer. Nessa will be pleased as well,' she added. 'She didn't like

42

Gabur much; everyone knows that. Gabur was twenty years older than she is, and he was ugly. Finbar is young and good-looking. Diarmuid will be jealous of Finbar, though; he's mad about Nessa.'

'Put everything out of your mind now,' said Flann. 'Go to sleep.'

Ita lay down obediently, but her dark-green eyes were wide and anxious.

'But, Father, what about Mahon?' she asked. 'What's going to happen to him now? I'm sure he didn't kill Gabur.'

Her father smiled. 'So it's Mahon your heart is set on,' he mused. 'Funny; I rather thought it would be Fergal. You're so alike, you and Fergal — both small and dark and serious. You'll both be good lawyers, too. I thought you would be able to carry on the law school after I'm dead. Still, we'll see what the future brings. There's plenty of time for you all.'

He kissed her and went out, leaving Ita rather confused and embarrassed. It was only later that she realised that he hadn't answered her question.

When she did eventually sleep, it was with that question still in the front of her mind: *What is going to happen to Mahon?*

And then another question kept coming to the foreground:

If Mahon didn't kill Gabur, then who did?

Chapter Six

It was a cold, damp day, six days before midwinter, when they buried Gabur. They laid him in a grave dug outside the bank of the fort at Caherblonick, where he had lived with his father and mother, and where his brother Colm still lived.

Finbar played the lament, his eyes resolutely fixed well away from the spot where Nessa stood, her red hair beautifully braided and a new green cloak wrapped around her tall figure. He plays wonderfully, thought Ita; she was glad of something to distract her from the sight of Gabur's body in the wet yellow clay, wrapped in his lawyer's robe, which was fastened with an elaborate gold brooch, and wearing a golden torc around his neck.

'That torc belonged to Gabur's father,' Fionnuala whispered in Ita's ear. 'He was a wicked, cruel old man, he was. Just like Gabur. He led his poor wife a dreadful life, and when she died, he carried on tormenting Colm. Colm's like his mother. A nice man. All these people here haven't come to pay their respects to Gabur; they've come out of liking for Colm.'

Ita looked around her. It was true, there was a large crowd there. Eithne had come with her son Lorcan, a big, powerful-looking young fellow. I wonder if she still hates Gabur now that he's dead, thought Ita. I would, if I were in her place. That was a terrible thing he did to her — shaming her and leaving her with a baby to look after.

There was a silence, and then once more Finbar lifted the horn to his lips. The final notes were piercingly high and sweet, and they echoed off the cliffs down by Poulnaboe, the hole where the River Fergus emerged from the ground after its mile-long journey underground. The water and the cliffs seemed to intensify the sound, making it almost unbearable. For some reason Ita felt like weeping. She turned and clutched Mahon's hand; he looked very white still, she noticed.

Then the last note of the horn died away, and Flann moved to the side of the grave.

'Colm's got no bard in his house; there'd be no one to deliver the eulogy about Gabur. Colm mustn't have wanted to do it himself, so the brehon must have offered,' whispered Fergal.

It's good, thought Ita, listening critically to her father's measured words. He said very little about what kind of man Gabur was and a lot about his achievements in the law — how clever he was, how many judgements he had won, how few he had lost. As Flann said that, Ita heard a mutter from behind her. She turned around. There, standing behind the law students, was the burly figure of Brendan of Kinvarra.

'What's he doing here?' she heard Owen whisper to Diarmuid. 'He doesn't live around here.'

'He's kin to Malachy at Ballycasheen,' whispered back Diarmuid. 'He must be staying with them.'

But why did he come to the burial? thought Ita. She looked around at the crowd huddled together, all eyes on the open grave. Fionnuala had said that the people came out of respect to Colm; but as Ita looked at the faces gazing down on Gabur's dead body, it was not respect she saw, but hatred — hatred, and a certain bitter pleasure.

She turned her eyes back to her father. He was still speaking.

'I sent to tell King Carthen about this untimely death, and he has sent back a message to say that a reward of ten ounces of silver will be given to anyone who discovers Gabur's murderer. The King will be at Coad in six days' time, on the last day of the midwinter festival, and he hopes that by then the matter will be settled.'

Everyone turned away from the figure in the grave and looked at Flann with a startled wariness in their eyes.

'Ten ounces of silver,' whispered Ninian. 'That would buy ten cows. There'll be a lot of people trying to discover the truth about Gabur's death.'

I suppose Father will be the one who finds out, thought Ita. He won't care about the silver — he doesn't really care about money; Fionnuala's always trying to get him to buy a new gown. He'll want to discover the truth, though. He has to, or else everyone will be accusing their enemies in order to get the reward.

'Everyone there hated Gabur,' she said to Fergal, as the seven of them walked back towards Drumshee.

Fergal nodded. 'Brendan,' he said.

'And Eithne,' chimed in Cathal.

'Shh,' said Diarmuid, with a glance at Ita.

'Oh, I know all about Eithne and Lorcan,' said Ita impatiently. 'Fionnuala told me. Lorcan is Gabur's son, but Gabur wouldn't acknowledge him.'

'And Lorcan, then,' said Cathal.

'And Donogh and Fionnuala, as well,' added Ninian seriously. 'Did you know Gabur was trying to get rid of them because he said Donogh's getting too old for the work? Owen told me that a few days ago.'

'I think everyone who knew Gabur hated him,' said Aidan. 'Except Ciarán, of course.'

'Ciarán?' questioned Mahon.

'Oh, I forgot you weren't there. Gabur gave Ciarán a piece of silver for knowing about feverfew curing headaches, and something else about the seeds of some flower — what was it, Ninian?'

'Foxglove,' said Ninian.

'Yes, foxglove. Ciarán told Gabur that foxglove seeds can kill a man, and Gabur gave him the silver, and so Ciarán liked him. But everyone else hated him.'

'And all of us, as well,' said Fergal thoughtfully. 'We all hated him.'

'Especially me,' said Mahon harshly.

There was a moment's silence. Cathal gulped noisily, and Diarmuid cleared his throat.

'The brehon will begin investigating tomorrow morning; he told me that last night,' he said. 'It'll all be cleared up soon. It might even have been an accident,' he added hopefully.

'Is he getting someone else to take Gabur's place?' asked Ninian.

'He's promised that Owen can have the place when he's passed his examination in the summer,' said Diarmuid. 'Until then, he'll manage on his own.'

'Well, that gives Owen a motive,' said Aidan. 'What do you say, lads? Owen's at the top of my list.'

Even Mahon laughed a little at that, Ita was glad to see. It was hard to imagine the gentle, studious Owen killing someone.

'What about Colm?' asked Ninian. 'After all, now he owns all the land that their father left. And he doesn't have to put up with his foul-mouthed brother shouting at him, like Ciarán told us about. I vote we put him on the list.'

'I suppose so,' said Fergal doubtfully. 'It doesn't seem like a very good reason, though. Colm must have plenty of silver and goods from his work as a physician, and I don't think he saw much of Gabur. Anyway, he wasn't anywhere near the Clab when Gabur was killed. He was at home, fast asleep.'

'I vote for it being an accident,' said Ita firmly. 'Let's all walk over to the Clab now, instead of going back to Drumshee. It's only about a mile. There won't be any lessons today, and we'll be back in plenty of time for dinner.'

'Yes, let's,' said Diarmuid resolutely. 'We have to find out what happened. Mahon said he didn't do it, and that's enough for me. I think we should all stick by him and get him out of trouble.'

'You don't mind going back there, Mahon, do you?' asked Fergal.

'No,' said Mahon. 'I minded more seeing him in the grave. Anyway, I keep going over it in my mind, trying to think what might have happened. He *was* killed, though, you know. It was no accident. I saw it all. Anyway, let's walk quickly, so we'll get there before it gets too late. I know a short cut past Malachy's place.'

'Is that Brendan's kinsman?' asked Cathal.

Mahon nodded. 'And Diarmuid's right, Brendan has been staying there. I saw him passing when I was hiding in ...'

'You'd better tell us where you were hiding,

Mahon,' said Fergal. 'It's no good telling lies. I'm sure the brehon knew. I know the way he twitches his eyebrow when he doesn't believe something.'

'I'll show you when we get there,' said Mahon, after a moment's pause. 'It's no big secret, really. Just sometimes when I get into a blazing temper I like to be on my own.'

After that no one said anything until they arrived at the place which they called 'the Clab'. It got its name from *clob*, the old country word for 'mouth'; and the hole did indeed look like a wide-open mouth, swallowing down the River Fergus and forcing it to run underground for more than a mile. The land here was limestone, very rocky and broken, with jagged cliffs and stone-filled holes, and a wide expanse of rocky shore just beyond the point where the river disappeared underground.

'He was there,' said Mahon, pointing at the stones. 'Just there, on that rocky bit.'

They all walked over.

'There's still blood on the stones, even after all the mist,' said Aidan with a shudder. 'Look, I can see it in that crack in the rock.'

'Could he have fallen?' asked Cathal. 'If his feet slipped from under him, he might have hit the back of his head hard enough to split his skull. I remember that happened to a man playing hurley at Tullagh.'

They all looked at one another with hope dawning in their eyes.

Diarmuid shook his head.

'I don't think so,' he said. 'I'm sorry, Mahon, but I don't think so. The whole of the back of his head was bashed in — and look, this is the stone that did it.'

With the toe of his boot he pointed to a long, narrow stone. There was no doubt about the blood on this stone; it was thickly encrusted with it. When Ita bent down to look, she could even see small pieces of bone sticking in the blood-clots.

She turned to Mahon. 'Where were you hiding?' she asked, trying to stop herself feeling sick.

'I was up there — you see the blackthorn bushes on the slope? Let's go up and I'll show you.'

They all climbed up the steep cliff. Mahon went ahead, behind the blackthorn bushes, and suddenly they could no longer see him.

'Just push aside the ivy,' came his voice.

Diarmuid reached out and moved the curtain of ivy. Mahon was in a small cave in the side of the cliff. The ivy and the blackthorn bushes had hidden it completely.

They climbed in. Mahon struck a light with a flint and some pieces of tinder, and in a moment he had a stump of candle lit.

'Fionnuala gave me these pieces of candle,' he said. 'How do you like the cave? Good, isn't it?'

'It's brilliant,' said Aidan enthusiastically. 'Does anyone else know about it?'

'Lorcan might,' said Mahon, after a pause. 'I've seen him scrambling around on the cliff over there to the south-west. He's never come here, though.'

'What about Nessa?' asked Ita. 'She lives quite near here.'

Mahon shook his head. 'Can you imagine Nessa climbing around cliffs? She's not that type at all. Her brothers might have known about it, but they're all grown up and married now. Anyway, have a look around.'

Chapter Six

They all explored the cave excitedly, and it was a
few minutes before they remembered what had
brought them there.

'Let's sit down,' said Diarmuid, taking charge as
usual. 'Now, Mahon, show us exactly where you
were that day.'

'Well, I was over here, standing looking out
through the bush. I was watching a hen-harrier. Its
wings were quite still; it was hovering over something — probably a shrew or something. And then I
saw him — Gabur, I mean.'

'What was the light like?' asked Ninian.

'It was sort of grey, really — a bit like today, but
of course it was much later. It was cloudy, but I think
it was just about sunset — I remember a bit of colour
in the clouds over there to the south-west, by that
cliff.'

'Go on,' commanded Diarmuid. 'What happened
next?'

'Well, I could see Gabur quite well; I could see
that he had a smile on his lips. He was laughing to
himself in that horrible —'

'You see what this means?' interrupted Fergal
excitedly.

'Let him finish,' said Diarmuid.

'You're quite right,' said Mahon. By the light of
the candle they could see a faint flush of hope come
over his face. 'I could see his face, and I was still
looking at it when there was a thud and he fell
forward. So the stone must have come from somewhere over there, over towards the south-west.'

'It must have been thrown by someone on top of
that cliff there,' said Fergal.

Mahon shook his head, looking puzzled. 'I don't

51

think so. You see, the sun set over that cliff, and I'd been looking at the clouds just a minute before Gabur appeared; I'd have seen anyone on top of the cliff.'

'Let's go down there, and you can show us again exactly where his body was lying. Then we can look up at the cliff and see if anyone could have flung a stone from there,' said Ita.

'I'll be Gabur,' said Aidan.

'And I'll throw the stone,' said Cathal.

'Shut up,' said Diarmuid. 'This isn't a joke; it's deadly serious for Mahon.'

Cathal hid his embarrassment by blowing out the candle. Aidan gave a quick grin, but said no more. They all climbed back down the cliff and onto the dry stone pathway which the River Fergus had carved out many thousands of years before it went underground.

'He came walking along here,' said Mahon. 'I thought he was going to Drummoher, to Nessa's place. He looked pleased about something; he was grinning to himself, like I told you. Then when he came to here, he stopped, and I heard a thud, and he fell forward on his face. I waited for a while, and then I came down and I saw the back of his head all smashed. I didn't touch him. I just ran back to Drumshee.'

'And you're sure you didn't see or hear anyone else?' asked Diarmuid.

Mahon shook his head. 'I'm sure,' he said.

'I think we should go back and tell my father about this,' said Ita. 'We'll bring him over and show him where Mahon was hiding, and he'll see that Mahon couldn't have thrown the stone. That is, of course....'

'That's if he believes me, you mean,' said Mahon with a bleak smile.

'We'll bring Owen as well,' said Fergal. 'He'll be able to say where Gabur's body was lying. Nobody touch anything. Come on, let's get back to Drumshee and bring the brehon out here before the light fades.'

🍀 Chapter Seven

They were all so excited that they covered the distance between Ballycasheen and Drumshee in record time. As they arrived at the gates they saw the small sandy-haired figure of Ciarán, Colm's apprentice, scuttle out of the pathway which ran down the hill from the Drumshee fort and shoot off in the opposite direction, towards Colm's home at Caherblonick.

'He's still afraid that I might hang him upside down so his brains will leak out on me,' said Aidan, and the seven of them were in such good spirits that they laughed hysterically at the joke.

'Hush,' said Fergal, who had sharp ears. 'There's a pony coming down the pathway.'

Everyone stopped laughing and listened. The pony was coming fast, far too fast for such a steep slope. Someone was riding at a desperate pace.

'It's Owen,' Cathal called out. 'Where are you going in such a hurry, Owen?'

Owen didn't reply. He gave a quick glance at Mahon; then he turned his eyes away, shot through the open gate and went galloping down the road.

'Well,' said Diarmuid, shutting the gate behind him. 'What's the matter with him? He looks like he's seen a ghost.'

And he looked at Mahon, thought Ita, a cold feeling coming over her. Something's wrong. I know it is.

'Here's another pony coming,' said Cathal. 'What's happening?'

This time it was old Donogh, trotting at a more leisurely pace.

'Where are you going, Donogh?' yelled Aidan at the top of his voice.

'To Colm,' said Donogh, in the toneless voice of the deaf. 'The brehon wants to see him urgently.'

'What about?' shouted Diarmuid in the old man's ear; but Donogh only smiled a toothless smile, shook his head at them and trotted on. Cathal ran back to open the gate for him, and they could hear him shrieking out the same question; but he came back shaking his head.

'Don't know what it's all about,' he said. 'It must be something urgent, for the brehon to send for Colm. After all, the man only buried his brother this morning.'

Ita stole a glance at Mahon. His colour had gone again, and his lips were set in a hard line.

'I'm not going back,' he said resolutely.

'Oh, come on,' she coaxed. 'It may be nothing to do with you at all.'

The six of them gathered around him.

'Come on, Mahon,' pleaded Fergal. 'We'll talk to the brehon. It will be all right, you'll see.'

Mahon shook his head. He ran his fingers through his rough brown hair and tried to say something, but a sob escaped him.

'You all go on up,' said Ita. 'Mahon and I will follow you. Don't say anything until we come.'

She waited until they had disappeared around the bend in the pathway. Then she held out her hand.

'Come on, Mahon,' she said. 'It may be nothing. You'll have to face it sometime.'

He shook his head again. He looked as if he was going to run away.

'I'll tell you what,' Ita said quickly. 'You wait here and I'll go up. I'll worm it out of Fionnuala, and then I'll come back and tell you. Will that do?'

Mahon nodded, and she began to run up the pathway. She guessed how he felt. She felt very worried herself. Something had happened.

The five boys were at the entrance to the enclosure when Ita arrived.

'Stay there,' she told them, in a whisper. 'I'll get it out of Fionnuala.'

Fionnuala was in the kitchen-house, boiling meat and cabbage for the evening meal. She looked pale and worried.

'Fionnuala,' said Ita, 'what's happened? Where's Owen going, and why has Donogh been sent to fetch Colm?'

Fionnuala turned around, and Ita was shocked to see that there were tears in the old woman's eyes.

'Colm's apprentice, Ciarán, came here to talk to the brehon,' she said.

'Ciarán!' exclaimed Ita. 'What's he doing talking to Father? He hardly has the courage to talk to us.'

'Oh, he has courage enough,' said Fionnuala bitterly.

'Go on,' said Ita impatiently. 'What did he say?'

'I don't rightly know. I wasn't there. The brehon took him into the schoolhouse.'

Ita waited. Very little got past Fionnuala. She would have been dying to know what business had brought Ciarán to talk to the brehon.

'Well, I was just passing,' began Fionnuala. 'And you know how that door doesn't fit very well....'

Ita nodded, afraid to say anything that might stop her.

'I heard Ciarán's voice, but I couldn't make out the words very well — he has that little whining voice, and it's hard to hear. But I heard the brehon very well. He was talking in a loud, angry voice. He said, "Are you telling me that you actually saw Mahon throw the stone at Gabur? Why didn't you say this before?" Ciarán said something and then the brehon shouted at him, "I suppose the ten ounces of silver have jogged your memory." And then, after a minute or two, he said, "Be off home with you now. If this is true, you'll get your silver." And Ciarán came out of the door and I went into the kitchen. Then the brehon came out and yelled for Owen to go and fetch Mahon's father, and for Donogh to ride over to Caherblonick and ask Colm to come over as soon as he could.'

'Oh, no,' said Ita with horror. 'Mahon is terrified of his father. That's the worst person to get.'

'Look, Ita,' said Fionnuala, 'this meat is ready. Get those boys in and we'll get a meal into Mahon before his father comes. Everything seems better when you have food inside you.'

'I'll call them,' said Ita, her mind numbed by the news. She went outside and walked over to the little group.

'Ciarán has told my father that he actually saw Mahon throw the stone at Gabur,' she said. 'My father has sent for Mahon's father and for Colm.'

'What!' said Cathal. 'It can't be true.'

'Of course it's not true,' flashed out Fergal. 'Don't be stupid, Cathal. Ciarán is making it up. He wants to get his hands on that silver.'

Ninian gave a long, low whistle.

'Of course,' he said. 'He's a mean little runt.'

'Don't say anything to Mahon,' said Ita. 'I'm going into the schoolhouse to talk to my father. Diarmuid, you and Fergal go and get Mahon and bring him in. Fionnuala has dinner ready. Tell him that I'm talking to the brehon and that everything will be fine.'

Diarmuid and Fergal shot off down the pathway, and Ita went across the enclosure and into her house.

It was quite dark in there, as no fire had been lit that day; and for a moment Ita thought that her father had gone. Then he raised his head and she saw his face gleam pale in the light from the door. Quickly she closed the door and sat down beside him.

'Father,' she said earnestly, 'don't believe Ciarán. He's a born liar.'

Flann sighed wearily. 'How did you find out? Don't tell me — Fionnuala, I suppose?'

Ita ignored this. 'Do you believe him, Father?' she asked urgently.

Flann sighed again.

'Ita, I neither believe nor disbelieve until I can get proof. I must talk to Mahon, but I have to wait until his father is here. It's not fair otherwise.'

At that moment Fionnuala came bustling in — ears flapping, thought Ita fondly. She was holding a small iron shovel laden with glowing pieces of turf.

'I'll light the fire for you, or you'll be destroyed with the cold,' she said.

Flann roused himself a little and held his hands out to the warmth.

'Ita, where's Mahon?' he asked.

'He's just started to eat his meal, poor lad,' said Fionnuala, with a warning glance at Ita.

'Well, let him eat,' muttered Flann, sighing again.

'Will you be wanting your dinner now, Brehon?' enquired Fionnuala. 'And what about Ita? Will she eat with you or with the lads?'

'Could you bring us over two bowls, Fionnuala?' said Ita quickly. Her father, she knew, seldom cared when he ate, but this would give her a bit of peace to talk to him.

Neither said a word until Fionnuala reappeared with two steaming bowls of meat and cabbage. Ita began to eat instantly. She, as well as Mahon, needed all her strength. Flann ate a few mouthfuls and then pushed his plate aside.

'I won't judge it myself,' he muttered. 'I'll ask King Carthen to send another judge. I'll act as lawyer for Mahon. He can still accept Colm's offer — but the King won't be happy with that. He may demand a greater penalty. It's a pity he's coming to Coad in a week's time. He'll want something to be worked out by then.'

Ita went on gulping down her dinner. Let him talk it out, she thought. He's not happy. He knows Ciarán isn't to be trusted; you only have to talk to Ciarán for two minutes to see that. And Fergal was right: Father always knows when people are lying.

'He's an honest boy, Mahon,' went on her father, still musing to himself. 'But he has a hot temper.'

'Father,' said Ita, 'what about Brendan? He had a reason to hate Gabur.'

'So you know about that, do you?' said Flann. 'Well, I suppose it's no secret. There wasn't much I could do about it; it was too hard to prove. Gabur was supposed to be selling some land for Brendan, and he persuaded him to take a very poor price for it;

and then, a few months later, it turned out that Gabur was the one who had bought the land. Brendan was furious. He came up here threatening to kill him. Gabur just laughed at him — you know that way he had, of laughing with all his teeth showing?'

Ita nodded. So that was why her father had asked, that night, whether Gabur had been killed. Perhaps he had expected Brendan to carry out the threat. Perhaps Brendan had. And perhaps, also, Flann was relieved to be rid of Gabur.

'Father ...' she began; and then she stopped as she heard the sound of ponies' feet on the cobbles outside. Panic seized her. That couldn't be Mahon's father already!

She ran to the door. Yes: there was Conall, large and surly as usual. Owen must have met him halfway. She would have to see Mahon quickly.

'Keep him talking for a moment, Father,' she said quickly. 'I must prepare Mahon.'

Without waiting for an answer, she ran over to the kitchen-house. It was too late, though. Diarmuid, Cathal, Ninian, Fergal and Aidan were standing at the front door, with Fionnuala trying vainly to peer over their shoulders; behind them, the back door was open, and there was no sign of Mahon anywhere.

'He's gone,' said Fergal. 'As soon as he heard his father, he was off.'

'Well, at least he has some dinner in him,' sighed Fionnuala.

'Sit down,' said Ita urgently. 'Go on with your dinner. Give him time to get away.'

They all sat down again. Through the open door, they heard a furious voice yelling, 'Where is the boy? Let me get my hands on him!'

Then they heard Flann's voice, but they couldn't make out what he was saying, no matter how hard they strained their ears. Then Conall's voice bellowed again: 'I met young Ciarán. He told me that Mahon killed Gabur.'

'No one knows anything, remember,' Diarmuid said fiercely.

When Flann appeared, a few minutes later, the boys were munching their way through a pile of honey-cakes and Ita was standing by the fire, talking to Fionnuala.

'Where is he?' asked Flann.

'Who?' asked Aidan, pretending to be puzzled.

Flann glared at him. 'Where's Mahon, Ita?' he demanded impatiently.

'I don't know, Father,' said Ita truthfully. 'He wasn't here when I came in.'

'I'll go look in the scholars' house,' said Cathal, diving through the door.

He was back after a long interval, shaking his head.

'I'll try the schoolhouse,' said Aidan solemnly, but with a quick wink at Ita behind his master's back.

Aidan was gone for a ridiculously long time; eventually he returned, shaking his head, but with a suppressed grin lurking behind his tightly closed mouth.

'I'll try the underground room,' offered Diarmuid, and sidled past Flann.

Maybe that's where he is, thought Ita, her heart lurching with terror. Most forts had underground rooms. Some, like the ones at Caherblonick and Drummoher, were part of the houses; but some, like the Drumshee underground room, were reached by steps going down from the centre of the enclosure. In the past, the Drumshee underground room had been used as a refuge from cattle raiders, but now it was mostly used to store great earthenware jars of oats. Perhaps Mahon had run down there when he heard his father's angry voice. For a moment she was panic-stricken.

Then her breathing steadied. Mahon wouldn't go there; it was too obvious a place. Anyway, even if he is there, Diarmuid won't betray him, she comforted herself.

In a few minutes Diarmuid was back.

'He's not there, Master,' he said solemnly.

'Let's try the stables, Fergal,' said Ninian. Both of their mouths were set in straight lines: they were obviously doing their best not to laugh.

This could go on for ever, thought Ita. But for some reason her father seemed content to stand and watch the game of 'Hunt Mahon' drag on. He's probably sorry that he sent for Mahon's father, she thought suddenly. He probably didn't realise what a violent man Conall is.

By the time Cathal came back from his fruitless search by the river, Flann had returned to Mahon's father. After a while they heard the angry man mount his pony and shout that he was to be sent for as soon as Mahon returned.

'Let me know when Mahon returns, Fionnuala,' said Flann, appearing at the door of the kitchen-house. 'Now, you others, you'd better do some studying. I'm afraid your lessons may be interrupted this week, as I have to prepare for King Carthen's coming to Coad. In any case, the midwinter festival starts in two days' time. You must work today. Come into the schoolhouse.'

They all trooped after him into the schoolhouse, and he took them through the Laws of Trespass at a brisk pace.

'The penalty when cattle break into meadowland is twice as much as when they break into rough moorland,' they all chanted obediently, their eyes fixed on the open window, wondering when Mahon would return.

At sunset Flann dismissed them, and still Mahon had not returned. The end of the day had been fine, and the sun went down in a blaze of glory in the western sky; and still Mahon had not returned.

Darkness had begun to fall when Flann and Owen came into the kitchen-house.

'We'll have to go and look for him,' said Flann decisively. 'Now come on, I'm sure you know his hiding-place. Where is he?'

They all looked at one another uncomfortably.

'Do you know, Owen?'

'No, Master,' said Owen earnestly.

Flann walked over to the door and looked out. The evening star, Venus, shone brightly in the south-eastern sky. He sniffed the air.

'It will be frosty tonight,' he said. 'That boy could die if he's out in the open all night. I'm sure that you younger ones know where he's hiding. Come on, now; I'm losing patience. Ninian! Where is he?'

'He might be in his cave, near the Clab,' muttered Ninian.

'Take a covered lantern, everyone,' ordered Flann. 'We'll go and get him. No ponies — they might slip in the frost and the dark. We'll walk.'

No one spoke on the two-mile journey. Ita was wondering what Mahon would say when he realised that his friends had given away his hiding-place; but, on balance, she was glad that her father had forced Ninian to tell. The evening was growing colder and colder; by the light of the lantern, she could see her breath hanging in a frosty cloud in front of her. It would be a bad night to spend in a damp cave.

When they arrived at the cave, however, there was no sign of Mahon. Flann held his lantern high and scanned the walls of the cave, but there seemed to be no other caves branching off from it.

'He mustn't have come here,' he said. 'Where can he be? He wouldn't have gone home, and he has no other kin near by. Any ideas?'

He did come here, thought Ita. She had known that the instant they came in. There were still spots of grease on the ledge near the entrance, but the box of candle-stumps that Fionnuala had given to Mahon had disappeared. He's been here, she thought; he came in, took the candles and went out again. Now where did he go, and why did he need candles?

'Show me the spot where Mahon found Gabur's body,' said Flann, breaking into her thoughts.

In silence they led him down the cliff and showed him the spot. By the light of the covered lantern, they could still see the black, clotted blood and the bits of bone on the heavy stone.

Flann nodded. 'Did Mahon say he saw anyone else around?' he asked, eyeing their faces keenly.

'Yes,' said Diarmuid hesitantly. 'He said he saw Brendan a while before Gabur.'

'How long before?'

Diarmuid shook his head. 'He didn't say.'

'And Gabur was struck down just about sunset? Mahon was sure of that?'

'Yes,' said Ita. 'Gabur was facing this way. Mahon could see a smile on his face, so the stone must have come from that cliff up there; but Mahon didn't see anyone there.'

'Perhaps Mahon wasn't looking in that direction,' said Flann thoughtfully.

'He must have been,' said Ita. 'The sun sets there, just behind that cliff. He said he was looking at the purple streaks in the clouds.'

'Well,' said her father, 'I'll see Brendan tomorrow, and I'll see what he has to say. Can anyone guess at any other hiding-place that Mahon might have?'

They all shook their heads. In the light from the lanterns, every face looked white and big-eyed. Could Mahon survive a night in the open? Or had he found shelter in some place that none of them knew about?

☘ Chapter Eight

Ita slept badly, haunted by nightmares of finding Mahon stiff and frozen on the rocky ground of the Clab. When she got up, she dressed and went over the icy flagstones to the kitchen-house. Fionnuala and Donogh were there; she knew that long before she reached the door. They were having a furious argument.

'You'll have to tell him,' Fionnuala was saying as Ita came near the door.

'Talk to Brendan, then,' replied Donogh, throwing open the door and pushing his way past Ita. His face was red and there was fear as well as anger in his eyes. For the first time in her life, Ita felt slightly afraid of him. Over the past few months he had been changing; there had been moments when she had wondered if he might be losing his mind. What will Fionnuala do if that happens? she wondered.

'Has Mahon come home yet?' she asked, going to the fire and holding out her hands to warm them.

Fionnuala shook her head. 'Not yet,' she said, stirring the porridge vigorously. 'I hardly slept a wink all night. I kept thinking I heard something....'

The five other boys and Owen trooped in. They glanced around quickly but said nothing.

Breakfast was a silent meal. When it was over, Flann came in; he, too, glanced around, but it was obvious that Mahon had not returned.

'Owen, I'll want you to go and fetch Brendan,' he said. 'Say nothing to him; just tell him I want to speak to him. When he comes, bring him in here.'

The students glanced at one another.

'Will we be present, Master?' asked Diarmuid.

Flann considered the matter. Eventually he nodded.

'Yes,' he said. 'As my students, you should be there. You're old enough now. Someday you will need to carry out this work yourselves, and you must learn how to do it. In any case, eight pairs of ears are better than two. After each witness, we will discuss the evidence. What you must remember is that the discussion takes place only among the members of the Drumshee law school; no outside person must know about what is said during these interviews. You understand that, all of you?'

He glanced around, and they nodded obediently.

'We understand, Master,' said Diarmuid firmly.

But Mahon is a student of the Drumshee law school, thought Ita. We'll be able to talk it over with him if we can find where he's hiding.

'Now,' said Flann briskly, 'while we're waiting, we must not waste your study-time. What have you been studying with Gabur?'

'The laws of kinship,' said Diarmuid, after a pause in which they all looked at one another blankly. It seemed such a long time since they had been taught by Gabur.

'Well,' said Flann, 'what is the meaning of *fingal*?'

'Easy,' said Ninian rapidly. '*Fingal* is the slaying of a kinsman.'

'And what is the penalty for *fingal*? What fine must be paid?'

'There is no fine sufficient for *fingal*,' said Ita.

That's a trick question, she thought.

'The penalty for *fingal* is banishment,' Cathal put in. 'The murderer is placed in a boat without oars and pushed out to sea. Even if he survives, he will never be allowed back to his own country.'

The rapid questions and answers went on. Ita hardly listened. They all knew this very well, and Ninian could be relied on to know anything that the others might have forgotten. The most important question was still going around and around in her head: if Mahon hadn't murdered Gabur, then who had?

Flann was running out of questions by the time that the sound of horses' hooves on the flagstones made them all turn their heads and stare at the door.

'Take your stools and sit over there in the corner,' ordered Flann. 'Say nothing, and listen carefully.'

They huddled on their stools in the dark corner that he indicated. Ita felt her heart beating faster; Diarmuid was twisting his fingers nervously, and every one of Cathal's freckles seemed to be standing out in his pale face. This was the first time they had been allowed to take part in a murder investigation; and their own friend was one of the suspects.

'Come in, Brendan,' said Flann, going to the door. 'Owen, ask Donogh to look after the horses, and then come and join us.'

Brendan was a big man; Ita knew that, but somehow she had never realised quite how huge he was until she saw him in that small room. He towered over Flann's slim, small-boned figure — a big man with huge, muscular arms and hands the size of small hams. His voice was large, like the rest of him, and it boomed out heartily in answer to Flann's polite apologies for taking up his time.

'No problem, Brehon, no problem. Delighted to do anything to help,' he said genially. His large forehead was damp with sweat, though, Ita noticed, and his massive hands opened and shut continuously. He was nervous; there was no doubt about it. He sat down on Flann's chair with a thud, then jumped up and apologised and took Owen's stool at the bottom of the table, balancing his large rear on it precariously and looking most uncomfortable.

'Sit here, Brendan,' said Flann firmly, indicating a chair placed opposite the window. Reluctantly Brendan moved to the chair, blinking as a ray of sunlight came through the window and lit up his large red face. It's not as red as usual, though, thought Ita. His bulbous, pimply nose was still a dark purple-red, but there were white patches on his flat cheeks, and drops of greasy sweat dripped down from his bulging forehead and filled the corners of his small eyes.

Owen came in, neat and unobtrusive as ever, and sat on his stool at the bottom of the table. Brendan took a piece of linen from his pouch and wiped his face, then turned to Flann.

'Terrible thing about Gabur,' he said, with an effort to appear at ease. 'And to think that I was only talking to him the very day he was killed.'

'What time was that?' enquired Flann.

'Must have been about midday,' said Brendan. 'I met him outside his brother's place at Caherblonick. We walked off together.'

'You were good friends, then,' stated Flann, his voice mild and neutral.

'Oh yes, best of friends,' said Brendan heartily, wiping his forehead once again.

Aidan dug Ita in the ribs, and Cathal gave a side-long glance at Diarmuid. Ninian frowned — he never could stand lies; Owen looked startled; but Flann's face was a mask, impossible to read.

'You walked off together,' said Flann. 'Where did you go?'

'Just walked,' said Brendan vaguely. 'You know — walked and talked, the way friends do.'

'But you weren't friends,' said Flann, and his words came as quickly as the sudden flash of a dagger from a sheath. 'You hated Gabur. He had cheated you out of the correct amount of silver for that piece of land you sold. You hadn't forgotten that, I'm sure.'

Ninian leant forward on his stool, his eyes shining. Fergal looked grave, and Ita felt a ripple of excitement run through her.

Brendan's mouth fell open and he gulped like a fish.

'You must have had a reason for going off with Gabur,' continued Flann rapidly. He was giving the slow-witted Brendan no time to think.

'Well....' said Brendan; and then he seemed to collapse. Once more he took out his piece of linen and mopped the sweat from his shining face.

'I'm thinking of marrying Eithne,' he said slowly. 'She's a decent woman, and I'm tired of living on my own and doing my own cooking and cleaning. But you know what Gabur did to her — you know how he lived with her and then left her on her own when she had a son?'

Flann nodded, his face expressionless.

'Well, I'm willing to look after Eithne, but Lorcan is a different matter. He's a big lad now. He wants to be a blacksmith, and Gowlaun the smith will take him and teach him if someone pays for him. But

Lorcan's not my son. Why should I pay for him? I asked Gabur if he would come with me and talk to Eithne. I told him that we were getting married. I didn't mention Lorcan. I thought that between us — Eithne and myself — we might be able to persuade Gabur to pay the apprenticeship fee, once I had him in Eithne's house.'

'And he went with you willingly?'

'He seemed to find it all a joke,' said Brendan. His voice deepened from its previous hearty, ingratiating tones, and now there was a note of anger — of rage, even — in it. Ita shivered. She looked at Fergal. His eyes were wide and his face had paled slightly. She knew him so well that she knew what he was thinking. This man, Brendan, was a man who could kill.

'And what happened when you got there?' asked Flann.

Brendan wiped his face again, and his hands, and then returned the piece of linen to his pouch. He seemed to be thinking hard.

'Well, we never got there,' he said eventually. 'You see, something happened on the way over.'

He stopped and Flann waited patiently, his face still showing no expression whatsoever. The others held their breath.

'You know that place where the old quarry is, down by the Isle of Maain?' went on Brendan slowly. 'Well, down there, just where the path rises, we saw young Finbar — you know, the horn player, the curly-haired fellow.'

He waited, but no one moved or said anything; so he went on, obviously thinking hard.

'Well, he was leaning against the rock, and in his arms — you couldn't mistake her, not with all that red hair — was Nessa, the girl Gabur was going to marry. She was in Finbar's arms, and he was kissing her and she was kissing him.'

Cathal's face flamed red enough to match his hair, and Ita felt herself flush as well. Aidan gave a quickly suppressed snigger, and Diarmuid bit his lips and turned as red as Cathal. Beside her Ita felt Fergal draw in a deep breath. A moment ago, we were all sure that Brendan killed Gabur, she thought; but now no one can be sure of anything.

'And what happened then?' Flann's voice was still dry and matter-of-fact.

Brendan took a deep breath, like a swimmer who sees that he is within reach of the shore.

'Well, Gabur shouted, and they ran, and Gabur took off after them, waving that big stick of his,' he said rapidly.

'And what did you do?'

Brendan blinked. The question seemed to take him by surprise, and he took a few moments to answer it.

'Me?' he said eventually. 'Well ... well, I just went home. I knew that it would be no good talking to Gabur any more that day,' he added lamely.

Flann raised his eyebrows. 'You didn't think to help Finbar?' he murmured.

Brendan took out his sodden piece of linen and once more wiped the sweat from his eyes.

'Well, Finbar is twenty years younger than either myself or Gabur,' he pointed out. 'I thought he could take care of it himself.' From behind the protective veil of his piece of linen, he shot a quick glance at Flann's face; then he wiped his neck and hands and returned the linen to his pouch.

Chapter Eight

There was a long silence.

'And you have no more to tell us?' said Flann gently.

'No, no more, Brehon. I didn't ever lay eyes on Gabur again until I saw him at his burial.'

Flann rose to his feet. 'You'll have something to eat and drink before you go back,' he said. 'Diarmuid, would you take Brendan to the kitchen-house and ask Fionnuala to look after him?'

Diarmuid jumped up and held the door open for Brendan, who hesitated and then followed him.

'Owen, go and fetch Finbar, and tell Donogh to fetch Nessa,' said Flann urgently. 'Both of you take spare horses. I want them here as soon as possible. Make sure that they have no opportunity to talk with Brendan.'

Owen shot off without hesitation, and Flann turned to his other students.

'Well?' he asked.

'He's a liar,' said Aidan instantly.

Flann's eyebrows shot up, and Ita winced.

'Why?' he said. Ita had known he would say that.

'Well ... well, he kept on sweating, and ... and it sounded like lies....' Aidan looked around at the others for help.

'You caught him out in a lie yourself, Master,' said Ninian. 'When he said that he and Gabur were great friends.'

'An improbability,' corrected Flann. 'I take your point, though.'

'I think,' said Fergal hesitantly, 'that the truth has to be proved in a court of law, but here, just among ourselves, we could admit that a lot of Brendan's statement seemed ... seemed improbable. Given that

73

he hated Gabur, it seems unlikely that he just walked away when Gabur went after Finbar and Nessa with his stick. Also, I think the fact that he kept sweating and looking uneasy would make me inclined to doubt his word, and at least to wonder about his evidence.'

'Excellently put,' said Flann. 'Well done, Fergal. I couldn't have put it better myself. Does everyone agree with this summing up?' He looked around. All heads were nodding; everyone looked relieved.

'And the next step is?' asked Flann.

'To test Brendan's evidence against what Finbar and Nessa say?' said Ninian rapidly. Flann nodded, looking satisfied.

'Will you see them separately, Master?' asked Diarmuid, who had just returned.

'Then you can test their evidence against each other's, as well,' said Ita, and again Flann nodded.

'You will be good lawyers one day,' he told them approvingly. 'Drumshee will be proud of you. Now you can have a break, but return as soon as Owen arrives with Finbar.'

~

It did not take Owen long to return with Finbar. Both of them dismounted in silence. Finbar looks worried and serious, thought Ita, as she joined the others in the schoolhouse. She had always rather admired him, and he sang beautifully; she didn't blame Nessa for preferring him to Gabur. I hope it wasn't Finbar, she thought.

'Thank you for coming, Finbar,' Flann was saying. 'I've just got a few questions for you — questions that I will be asking of everyone around here. On the day that Gabur was murdered, did you see him at any time?'

Finbar looked around him nervously and licked his dry lips.

'Which day was that, Brehon?' he asked after a minute's pause.

That's stupid, thought Ita scornfully. He must remember. He was at the burial.

'On Saturday,' said Flann, his tone polite and helpful.

'Saturday....' Finbar pretended to think hard. 'No, I ... I can't remember.'

Aidan pursed his lips in a silent whistle and Ninian sighed impatiently. Diarmuid looked scornful. He hasn't given up hope of winning Nessa himself, thought Ita, and he's glad that Finbar's shown himself to be so slow-witted. She looked at her father, but Flann's face showed nothing.

'I'm not good at remembering days,' said Finbar, looking around him for help. 'I might have done.'

He looked hard at Owen. They were about the same age; they weren't friends, but they knew each other. Finbar obviously hoped Owen would give him some clue.

But Owen just stared at the table, and Finbar's cheeks turned a delicate shade of pink. His blue eyes were full of misery, and he ran his fingers through his brown curls a few times.

Ita began to feel very sorry for him. She looked at her father indignantly. Why didn't he just come straight out and ask Finbar if Brendan had told the truth?

There was a clatter from outside and then the sound of Donogh's toneless, over-loud voice.

'That, I think, must be Nessa,' said Flann. 'Ita, would you go out and tell Donogh to fetch Eithne and Lorcan now? Look after Nessa for a few minutes. We'll send for you when we're ready.'

Ita got up from her stool and slipped out of the door. Her last impression was of Finbar's blue eyes filled with alarm — and something else, as well. Could it be true? Could it be that he looked terrified?

Nessa looks frightened too, thought Ita, as she went to greet her after giving Donogh the message.

'What's happening, Ita?' she exclaimed. 'Was that Brendan I saw riding away from here? What does the brehon want with me? My father will kill me if he hears anything.'

If he hears what? thought Ita. But she was sorry for Nessa. Everyone knew that her father was a bad-tempered brute. Nessa had only agreed to marry Gabur because she was so frightened of her father. Nessa was so beautiful, with her grown-up figure, her masses of red hair rippling to her waist and her beautiful amber eyes — it was no wonder that Diarmuid, as well as Finbar, was so in love with her. She looked years older than Ita, although she was actually only a year older. She was very tall; Ita had to look up at her.

The two girls stood in silence for a moment, and still Ita said nothing. Then, suddenly, Nessa wrenched a small stone from the top of the encircling wall around the enclosure. With fiercely accurate aim, she flung it at a grey crow who was picking up leather-jacket grubs from the muddy soil. The crow rose into the air with an indignant squawk.

'I don't care!' Nessa exclaimed. 'I don't care what happens now. At least I don't have to marry that old man Gabur. It made me sick to look at him!'

Ita didn't know what to say. Was Nessa — were Nessa and Finbar responsible for Gabur's death? And if they were, did she want them caught and punished?

Then a picture of Mahon, hiding out in the cold like an outlaw, came to her, and her own words to her father echoed in her mind: 'The law is there to find the truth.' That was what she had said, and she had to stick to it.

She looked at Nessa calmly and wondered about the girl who had once been her friend. Still, she said nothing and gave Nessa no help. They had to find the truth.

'You're to come in now,' said Diarmuid, appearing at the door and smoothing his blond hair with his hand. His face was pink at the sight of Nessa, but she didn't give him a second glance; she just walked past him like a queen. Ita followed and sat down on her stool in the corner. Owen quickly offered Nessa his seat and found himself another stool.

'We've been talking about the day Gabur was killed,' said Flann gently. 'I wonder, Nessa, is your memory of that day the same as Finbar's? Perhaps you could tell me what you remember about your meeting.'

Finbar had said nothing, Ita was sure of that. His mouth opened quickly, but then shut as Nessa spoke.

'I was with Finbar,' she said coldly. 'We were down at the Isle of Maain. Gabur came along with Brendan, and he saw us ... he saw us kissing,' she finished, lifting her chin and staring defiantly at Flann.

'And what happened then?' asked Flann in a level, unconcerned voice.

'Well, you can guess,' replied Nessa, her voice

harsh. 'Gabur went mad — he considered me his property. He came charging up like a wild bull, and he hit me across the back with his stick and screamed that he would order my father to beat me and that he would make my life a misery once we were married.'

'And what did you do, Finbar?' Flann's words came so quickly that Finbar gasped and sat for a moment with his mouth hanging open.

Nessa looked at him for the first time since she had entered the room, and her glance was proud and possessive. She reached across the table and took his hand in hers. The colour had drained from Finbar's cheeks, and he moistened his lips twice and ran his hand through his curly brown hair before he replied.

'I ...' he stuttered, 'I didn't do anything. He walked away right after hitting Nessa. I thought it was best just to let him go.'

He took his hand from Nessa's and looked around the room. Flann's face, as usual, was impossible to read, but all the boys had their mouths open in astonishment, and Diarmuid had flushed a furious fiery red. It does seem unbelievable, thought Ita, that a strong young man would let another man hit the girl he loved and do nothing in return! Her opinion of Finbar began to go down. Nessa had more courage than he.

The strange thing was that Nessa was still looking at Finbar with that proud, possessive look. Surely she should be ashamed of him if he had done nothing to protect her from Gabur?

'And did Gabur come to see your father?' Flann asked Nessa.

She looked him straight in the eye. 'No, my lord,' she said. 'He never arrived.'

~

'I just don't believe it,' burst out Aidan, as soon as
Finbar and Nessa left. 'I know there's no evidence
that they're lying, but I just don't believe that nothing
else happened.'

'Let's say that the probability is strong that something did happen,' said Ninian. Ita noticed that her
father looked amused. Ninian was very inclined to
imitate his master.

'What do you think, Father?' she challenged, looking
at him directly.

'I think that Ninian put it rather well,' he said
thoughtfully. 'Now go and have your dinner, all of
you. We'll go through the evidence again after that.'

'What about Mahon?' said Ita, when dinner was
over and they had gone over and over Brendan's and
Finbar's and Nessa's evidence. 'Should we look for
him again? Maybe he's hurt.'

'We'll form two parties,' ordered Flann. 'Owen,
you take Ita and Fergal and Diarmuid, and search
around the Clab. Aidan, Cathal, Ninian and I will
search the Isle of Maain area.'

Ita was the first into Mahon's secret cave at the
Clab. Desperately she hoped that she would find him
there. She raised the lantern high as Owen and the
others came in.

'Well, he's not here,' said Owen. Ita said nothing.
She was looking at a footprint in some damp clay
near the back of the cave. It hadn't been there the
day before, she was sure of that; she had examined
that part of the cave very carefully when her father
had been looking for a way out at the back.

The footprint wasn't very large — it could have been made by any of the boys; but what caught her attention was the uneven pattern of nails on the sole of the boot. She remembered sitting with Mahon one day as he mended his boot and laughing at the random way he set the nails.

Mahon had been there sometime during the day. He was alive, and he was hiding somewhere nearby.

Will he still be alive tomorrow morning? wondered Ita, as they went home in the last rays of the winter sunset.

Chapter Nine 🌺

The next morning, just before sunrise, Ita was woken by a faint noise at her window.

It must be a bird, she thought sleepily — some poor half-frozen bird looking for insects in the wooden frame of the window. She shook herself awake, wrapped her cloak around her, went to the window and opened the shutter.

During the winter a piece of oiled linen was nailed over her bedroom window, so that light, but not too much wind, could come in during the daytime. A long strip of wood had been pushed under the linen and was sticking into the room. Wide awake now, Ita pulled it out and held it up to the first rays of sun in the frosty sky.

Immediately she saw that some signs were carved into the wood in Ogham, the writing which all law students learned. The piece of wood was a message, and instantly Ita knew that it had come from Mahon. He was very proud of his ability to write Ogham and was always practising it.

Slowly, letter by letter, she spelt out the message.
I am at the Clab, it said. *Come there at sunset.*

'Great!' Ita said aloud. Mahon had survived the two nights; she should have known that he was practical and sensible. Now she needed to get food and, if possible, some bedding to him. Let him stay in hiding until his name was cleared. There were others who had just as much reason to kill Gabur, and her father would uncover the truth — she was confident of that. Hastily she began to dress, putting on her woollen tunic and stockings and adding the thick cloak on top of everything else.

'I've heard from Mahon,' she whispered to the others, as they all crowded around the fire in the kitchen-house, waiting for Fionnuala to pour out the bowls of porridge.

'What?'

'How?'

'Where is he?' They all crowded around her, and cautiously she showed them the message on the piece of wood. Behind them, Fionnuala paused in the act of pouring the porridge from the wooden jug.

Ita decided to take a chance. They would need Fionnuala's help if they were going to feed Mahon properly. She crossed to the table and slipped an arm around the old woman.

'Fionnuala, if you met Mahon, would you tell anyone where he was?' she asked coaxingly.

'You know I wouldn't,' said Fionnuala indignantly. 'Have you heard from him?'

Ita nodded. 'Fionnuala, I must get food for him. I'm going to meet him at sunset.'

'I'll get you something for him. Poor lad! It's a shame. I'm sure he did nothing. He's not the only one that wanted Gabur dead. There's plenty know more than they're saying about Gabur's death.'

'What do you mean?' asked Cathal, but Fionnuala only shook her head and pursed up her lips as if she had said more than she had intended. Ita gave the boys a warning glance. She would get more out of Fionnuala when she was alone with her.

Chapter Nine

'Could we have an old sheepskin or something for Mahon?' asked Fergal. 'He must be very cold at night.'

'What about a couple of bales of hay?' suggested Fionnuala. 'Donogh will be taking hay to the cows today in the horse-cart. I could get him to drop off a couple of bales in a handy place.'

The students exchanged glances. Fionnuala they could trust; could they trust her husband also?

She seemed to guess their thoughts. 'Not too near where he's hiding,' she said hastily. 'The fewer people who know that, the better.'

'By the roadside beyond Drummoher, just by the lane to the old burial mound,' said Ita. 'No one goes near that place. Tell him to leave it there about noon.'

'Hurry up with your breakfast,' said Flann, opening the door of the kitchen-house. 'I want to do some work with you before Eithne and Lorcan arrive.'

So that's who it is today, thought Ita. I wonder, did Eithne know that Brendan wanted to bring Gabur to see her? Did she really want to marry that fat, loud-mouthed Brendan?

Quickly she gobbled down her porridge and sent a glance around the table, warning the others to do the same. It was important to keep her father in a good humour. She intended to beg a half-holiday for them after the morning's work was over.

~

'Honour-prices,' announced Flann, as soon as they were all sitting on their stools in the schoolhouse. 'Honour-prices are one of the most important things

for you to learn about in Brehon Law,' he said slowly
and impressively. 'Have I your attention, Aidan?'

'Yes, Master,' said Aidan, hastily turning his eyes
from the door, where he could see Owen mounting a
pony and riding off.

'All fines and penalties depend on a man's honour-
price,' went on Flann, 'and the honour-price is fixed
by the man's land or by his trade or profession.'

'Or the woman's,' said Ita.

Flann ignored her. 'Now I want to test you on
them,' he continued. 'Cathal, what is the honour-
price of a physician?'

'Three and a half ounces of silver, or three and a
half cows,' said Cathal.

'Would the half-cow be a dead cow or a living
cow, Master?' enquired Aidan, with a bland face and
a grin lurking at the corners of his mouth.

'Shut up, Aidan,' muttered Diarmuid.

'We'll omit the cows,' said Flann gravely. 'Just
answer in *séts* and ounces of silver. Aidan, what's the
honour-price of a chariot-maker?'

That's a hard one, thought Ita. There aren't too
many chariot-makers around. And in *séts*, too.... The
sét was a unit of value worth half an ounce of silver,
but not many people bothered with it these days.

I suppose a chariot-maker's honour-price might be
the same as an ordinary craftsman's, she thought.
Yes, it would be.... Quickly she put her hands flat on
the table and doubled back all her fingers except
three. She glanced at Ninian with her eyebrows
raised; he gave a half-nod. That was right, then.

'Three *séts*, or one and a half ounces of silver,'
said Aidan, glancing at the table and then quickly
averting his eyes from Ita's hands.

'Good,' said Flann. 'Diarmuid, what is a silver-wright worth?'

'Seven *séts*, or three and a half ounces of silver.'

'Good again. Ita, the honour-price of a harpist?'

'Five *séts*, or two and a half ounces of silver,' said Ita. If Finbar had been a harpist, rather than a horn player, would Dara have allowed him to marry Nessa? she wondered. Maybe Gabur wouldn't be dead if Finbar had been a harpist.

The more she thought about it, the more possible it seemed that Finbar had followed Gabur and killed him. After all, it was fairly unlikely that a strong young man like Finbar would let someone hit the woman he loved with a stick and not try to revenge himself. Had Finbar followed Gabur and slung a stone at him?

She sighed and dragged her mind back to the schoolroom. Fergal had just answered a question, and her father looked satisfied. Fergal must have got it right; he was always careful.

'You may have your break now,' said Flann at last. 'All right, Cathal, you may play hurley. Come back as soon as you see Donogh arrive with Eithne and Lorcan. Their evidence will probably take up most of the morning. In the afternoon ...'

'Could we search for Mahon?' asked Ita quickly.

Flann hesitated. 'Remember, the next three days are holidays,' he said. 'Tomorrow is the first day of the midwinter festival at Coad. I don't want you to get behind with your studies.'

'Please, Father,' said Ita. 'He must be very cold and hungry by now.'

She tried to keep her voice steady, but it shook as she thought of Mahon.

Flann looked at her gently. 'Yes, you can all have the afternoon free in order to look for him,' he said. 'Don't worry too much about him. He's a brave, clever lad. He'll be all right.'

'Funny, isn't it,' said Aidan, after Flann had gone out. 'The master said Mahon is clever, but Gabur was always calling him stupid.'

'My father's right,' said Ita. 'Mahon is clever, but he's clever in a different way from the way Ninian is clever.'

'Or Ciarán,' added Aidan, and that got the laugh he was looking for.

In fact, they were all feeling quite cheerful. At least Mahon was alive, and well enough to come over to Drumshee and put the message in at Ita's window. They would see him that afternoon and give him food and bedding, and then they would all plan what to do.

'Let's have a quick game of hurley, then,' said Diarmuid, taking charge as usual. 'We'll have time before Donogh gets back. Will you play, Ita?'

'No,' said Ita. 'I think I'll slip into the kitchen-house and talk to Fionnuala. I'm sure she knows more than she's said. Do you remember what she said this morning? She said, "There's plenty know more than they're saying about Gabur's death." I'll try and get something more out of her. And another thing: I heard Donogh and Fionnuala having a big argument about something. Fionnuala was saying that Donogh should tell what he knows. They never argue normally. And remember, Donogh went out the evening when Gabur was killed.'

'Donogh!' said Aidan. 'Never! He's too old and silly.'

'He might know something, though,' said Ita thoughtfully. 'And if he does, Fionnuala will have got it out of him by now.'

Ita waited until the boys had gone off with their hurley sticks, all shouting happily. Then she slipped into the kitchen.

Fionnuala smiled at her. 'Getting too big for boys' games now, are you?' she asked.

Ita shook her head. 'No,' she said. 'I just can't enjoy myself while I'm thinking about Mahon. Fionnuala, do you think he killed Gabur?'

'No, I don't,' said Fionnuala stoutly.

'But you did, that night — the night he found Gabur's body.'

Fionnuala fidgeted a little. 'That was different. I suppose I hadn't had time to think.'

'Or you hadn't heard something that you heard later on,' said Ita shrewdly.

Fionnuala picked up a sharp knife and began chopping the cabbage. It's going to be nothing but water if she cuts it as small as that, thought Ita, watching the busy knife cutting the cabbage into smaller and smaller pieces.

Eventually, Fionnuala swept the pieces off the wooden table and threw them into the iron pot over the fire, took down a piece of salted bacon from the beam that ran across the kitchen ceiling, slashed a generous chunk off the bacon and tossed that into the pan as well. She wiped her hands on her skirt, and then turned and faced Ita.

'Never tell anyone that I told you,' she began. 'And make sure you keep Donogh's name out of this, won't you? He's getting to be an old man now, and he's a bit silly, but he wouldn't hurt a fly.'

Ita nodded. Left to himself, Donogh wouldn't hurt a fly, she knew that; but she also knew that he would follow any orders given to him, by Fionnuala or by anyone else.

'Brendan came here and talked to Donogh that day,' said Fionnuala in a fierce whisper, with her eye on the door. 'Donogh went off after him. He went to Cahermacon, where Brendan's kinsman Malachy lives. Brendan told him that they were going to sort Gabur out — do something about him, stop him injuring everyone, stop him spoiling people's lives.'

'They?' asked Ita. 'Brendan and Donogh?'

Fionnuala shook her head. 'No, many more than that. I got it out of Donogh. "Who was at that house?" I asked him, and he told me, in the end. Finbar was there, and so was Nessa; and Eithne was there, and Lorcan with her; and Brendan and Donogh and Brendan's kinsman Malachy.'

Ita waited, a feeling of horror creeping over her. Had they all killed Gabur?

'What happened?' she said finally.

Fionnuala shook her head. She had a slightly puzzled look on her face. 'Donogh said that nothing happened,' she said. 'Of course, he couldn't really hear what they were talking about, he's that deaf; but Brendan told him to go home, and to meet him at noon the next day in the Isle of Maain. That's all he knows.'

'Was he the first to go home?' asked Ita.

Fionnuala nodded gravely. 'He went home first. All the others were just sitting there when he left.'

She turned back to her cooking-pot, with the air of someone who had said more than she intended.

Ita wandered out to the gate of the enclosure and

looked out at the field where the boys were playing. Cathal had just shot a goal. Every head turned when they saw her, and they trooped over.

'Quick,' said Diarmuid, brushing the mud from his tunic. 'They're coming; I hear the ponies. Did you get anything out of Fionnuala?'

'Yes,' said Ita, and as rapidly as possible she told them the whole story. 'My father will have to know about this,' she finished, 'but I don't know how to tell him without telling him that Fionnuala told me.'

'Wait until tomorrow,' advised Fergal. 'We can tell him when we get back from the fair at Coad. We can tell him that we heard it at the fair, and if he asks who said it, we can just say, "Well, you know what it's like at Coad at this time of the year, Master. It's full of people, and most of them are strangers." He won't press us; I know that.'

'That's clever,' said Ita approvingly. 'We'll do that. Let's go in now and tell him that Eithne and Lorcan are coming.'

~

Eithne doesn't look like the sort of woman who would make Gabur, or any other man, fall in love with her, Ita thought as mother and son came into the schoolhouse. Nessa was tall and beautiful, with lovely hair and lovely eyes; but Eithne was small and squat, with pale-grey eyes, dull brown hair and a muddy complexion. Her shoulders were hunched and her mouth was sour and pinched. Lorcan looked a little like her, but Fionnuala was right: he did also look like Gabur. He did have the same teeth and the same shape of head.

Flann treated Eithne as if she were a queen, making sure that she was warm enough and that she did not want any refreshments before answering the questions; but Eithne's mouth remained sour and her eyes were dark with suspicion. She took her seat at the table and Lorcan stood behind her, refusing Owen's offer of a stool.

'We're trying to find out who was the last person to see Gabur alive,' explained Flann.

Eithne said nothing; she just waited for him to go on.

'Did you see him on the day he was killed?' Flann enquired, after a moment's pause.

'No, my lord,' said Eithne.

'When did you last see him?'

Eithne hesitated. 'I don't know, my lord. Not for a long time.'

'But you knew him?'

Eithne hesitated again. 'I knew him, my lord, but not well.'

Ita felt Aidan, beside her, draw in a breath, and saw Cathal and Diarmuid glance at each other from the corners of their eyes.

There was another long pause. Flann looked hard at Eithne, and Eithne looked dully ahead of her.

'But you once knew each other very well indeed,' said Flann. 'It is no secret that you and Gabur lived together for years and only parted some months before Lorcan's birth.'

'Shut your mouth!' screamed Lorcan. 'Leave her alone, you —'

He didn't finish his sentence; instead, he seized the heavy oak table with both hands and tipped it dangerously towards Flann. Diarmuid and Aidan jumped to their feet and threw their weight onto the table, Owen grabbed Lorcan by the shoulders and the other boys ran to help Owen.

'Sit down,' ordered Flann. Owen brought his stool and pushed Lorcan down onto it.

'Go back to your places, boys,' said Flann quietly. His green eyes watched Lorcan intently.

'What about you, Lorcan?' he asked. 'Did you see Gabur that day?'

Eithne reached out and touched her son on the arm. He shrugged her off, his face sullen.

'Did you?' persisted Flann.

Still there was no answer.

'You knew him, of course, didn't you? You must have known him. Your mother claimed that he was your father. You were fond of him?'

How can he say such things? thought Ita.

Then, suddenly, a terrible sound burst from Lorcan's lips. It was halfway between a scream and a wail. A torrent of the most obscene language Ita had ever heard poured out of him.

The other boys looked at one another uneasily. Ita looked at her father. He never allowed any of the boys to utter even the mildest of swear-words in front of his daughter; but now he sat like a cat at a mouse-hole — he sat and watched Lorcan intently, and listened to him pour out a litany of hate.

Ita began to feel sick. It was not the swearing that upset her so much as the terrible hate behind the words.

'So you didn't like Gabur.' Flann's quiet voice cut across the hysterical shriek. 'You could not wish him dead, though, could you?'

Eithne rose to her feet and rushed to the end of the table. 'Lorcan!' she screamed, but it was too late.

'He deserved it,' said Lorcan, a froth of spittle fringing his lips. He jumped to his feet and crashed his fist down on the table with a blow that rocked Owen, who was trying to hold on to him. 'We all agreed on it: he deserved it.'

'We?' queried Flann. He was the only calm one in the room. Even Ninian was on his feet.

'Be quiet, Lorcan!' cried Eithne.

'Who's "we"?' asked Flann again. 'Or do you mean "I"?' he added.

Eithne faced him. Colour had flooded into her face and her eyes flashed. Suddenly Ita could see the remnants of beauty in this drab middle-aged woman.

'My lord,' she said, 'take no notice of him. My son is only a child. This is just wild boy's talk. I'll tell you everything that happened on the day Gabur was killed.'

Suddenly all the tension in the room collapsed. Ita leant back against the wall, feeling weak and trembling; Lorcan buried his face in his outstretched arms; Ninian sat down, and the others came back to their stools. The room became very quiet.

'Gabur did great harm to all of us around here,' began Eithne, her low, harsh voice sounding calm, almost indifferent. 'He left me without a man to care for me; he left my son without a father; he cheated Brendan; he beat Nessa in front of the man who loves her; he was forcing this marriage on her; he threatened Donogh.

'Brendan knew all of those things. He persuaded Finbar to do nothing, and he organised a meeting at Cahermacon, the place belonging to Malachy, his kinsman. During that meeting, it was decided that Brendan would bring Gabur to the Isle of Maain on

Sunday morning, and that all of us would take part in beating him. We decided that he would be beaten until he agreed to care for Lorcan, to return Brendan's silver, and to give up his claim to Nessa.'

'And that was to take place on Sunday morning — not on Saturday evening?' asked Flann, his keen eyes probing hers.

'On Sunday morning, my lord,' insisted Eithne.

'But by then he was dead?'

'By then he was dead,' she repeated.

'And after the meeting ended, you all went home? Together?'

'No, my lord, we all went our separate ways. But neither Lorcan nor I ever saw Gabur alive again.'

Chapter Ten

The two bales of hay were lying on the ground near the burial mound beyond Drummoher when they got there that afternoon. Mahon had told them to be there at sunset, but they arrived shortly after noon. It would take them some time to drag the hay over to the Clab; and there was a chance that Mahon was hiding nearby and would see them, and then they would have more time to spend with him.

However, the road to the burial mound wasn't deserted as usual. Standing beside the two bales of hay was a small figure with sandy-red hair and eyes the colour of boiled gooseberries.

'What are you doing here, Ciarán?' said Cathal roughly. 'Clear off.'

'I'm wondering why Donogh dropped these bales of hay here,' said Ciarán innocently. 'He did it on purpose. I saw him. He stopped the cart and took off the backboard and pushed the bales off, and then he put back the backboard, turned the horse around, and went back again.'

'I think my father's going to rent some land from Nessa's father,' said Ita hastily. 'Donogh is probably dropping off the hay before he brings the cows over.'

I'm getting very good at telling lies, she thought. Still, the last thing we want is that little spy guessing Mahon's hiding-place.

'What are you doing here anyway, Ciarán, you little rat?' asked Diarmuid.

'Come here often, do you?' asked Aidan. 'Maybe you were here the other day, when Gabur was killed just over there at the Clab. Maybe you were hiding somewhere and you killed him with your sling.'

'I didn't,' said Ciarán, alarmed.

'I bet you did,' said Ninian. 'You were the one who killed him, and that was why you made up the lie about Mahon. Don't think that you're going to get your greedy little hands on that ten ounces of silver. The brehon knows you were lying. Now we're going to go back and tell him that you were the one who killed Gabur, and then we'll get the ten ounces of silver.'

Ita looked on, amused. They were diverting Ciarán from the question about the bales of hay.

'Show us your sling,' said Diarmuid, joining in the game.

'I don't have a sling,' said Ciarán quickly.

'Show us your pouch,' ordered Fergal.

Ciarán opened his pouch, smiling smugly. There was nothing in it but a piece of snow-white linen, folded neatly.

'Wait a minute,' said Cathal. 'You do have a sling. I remember seeing it. You showed it to me once. It was made from ram's hide, and it had a patch of white hair on it.'

'I lost it,' said Ciarán, after a minute.

'I bet we find it up on the cliff above the Clab. Then we'll be certain that Ciarán killed Gabur,' said Aidan.

'No, I didn't!' shrieked Ciarán. 'I know where my sling is. I've just remembered. It's in the herb garden.

I was cleaning it with the soapwort plant the day Gabur was killed. I never had it near the Clab. Don't say anything to the brehon about my sling! I'll go to him myself. I'll tell him I made a mistake. I'll tell him I didn't really see Mahon kill Gabur.'

Turning his back, he scuttled off like a scared rabbit.

'Well, that got rid of him,' said Diarmuid with a grin. 'Give him another minute, and then we'll haul the hay up to the Clab.'

There was no sign of anyone when they reached the Clab. They stood at the spot where Gabur's body had been found and looked around. Fergal whistled, a long, melodious note.

For a moment nothing happened; then they heard a stone roll down the slope of the cliff, on the south-western side. Quickly they all turned. A rough, brown-haired head had appeared halfway up the cliff-side, and an arm beckoned to them.

'He must have found another cave up there,' said Ita. 'We should have thought of that. Where there's one cave, there are usually several.'

'Look all around, carefully,' said Diarmuid. 'Check there's no one watching before we climb up there.'

They waited a few minutes, checking in every direction, but there was no one around. Quickly they began to climb the steep cliff. Diarmuid and Cathal were carrying the bales of hay on their backs; Fergal and Ninian carried leather buckets which held honey-cakes, porridge, hunks of oaten bread, slices of cold bacon, and everything else Fionnuala could think of. Aidan had a bag with a covered lantern and some fresh candles, so that Mahon wouldn't have to sit in the dark, and Ita carried an old cloak of her father's.

It was threadbare in places and had been torn by a brooch-pin, but it was still thick and warm and would make a good cover for Mahon's hay bed.

They had been right: Mahon had found a second cave. It was smaller than the first one, but it seemed drier. Mahon looked tired and dusty but otherwise quite well. He fell on the porridge and cold bacon and ate ravenously.

'I managed to steal a few eggs from Drummoher,' he said. 'But those, and some watercress from the river, are all I've had to eat for the last two days.'

They watched him in silence while he ate his fill. Finally he sat back with a sigh and wiped his mouth.

'Look out of the mouth of the cave,' he said. 'Do you think what I think?'

They looked out, and all six heads nodded.

'You mean that whoever murdered Gabur was hiding here,' said Ita, putting their thoughts into words.

'Yes,' said Mahon. 'It's just right. The stone came from here and hit him on the back of the head, and he fell forward. There was still plenty of light. The murderer would have known that he was dead.'

'He must have seen you go down and look at Gabur, I suppose, and then he saw you run off, back to Drumshee. By the time Owen arrived, he would have been well gone,' said Fergal.

'Who was it, though?' asked Mahon despairingly.

'Wait till you hear!' said Ita.

'We've lots to tell you,' said Diarmuid. 'The master is questioning everyone, and we've been there all the time.'

'Go on, Ninian,' said Ita. 'You tell him. You're good at explaining complicated things.'

Ninian rose and bowed, and put the tips of his

fingers together just as Flann did when he explained some complex point of law.

'I'll go through the names one by one,' he said. 'First we'll take Brendan.'

'The big fat man from Kinvarra,' explained Aidan.

'Exactly,' said Ninian pompously. 'Well, Brendan had another motive for murdering Gabur, as well as revenging himself on Gabur for cheating him over that land deal. Unlikely as it seems, Brendan wanted to marry that dreary Eithne, and he wanted Lorcan, her equally dreary son, off his hands. He hoped he could persuade Gabur to recognise Lorcan as his son, and to pay to apprentice Lorcan to Gowlaun the blacksmith; but he may well have given up on this, knowing what Gabur was like. But yesterday the master told Eithne that he'll get the King to provide for Lorcan out of Gabur's lands. He said Colm had agreed. Now, it's possible that Brendan worked that one out for himself. He might have thought that if Gabur were dead, Colm might provide for Lorcan.'

'And, Mahon,' said Ita excitedly, 'Brendan and Finbar and Nessa and Eithne and Lorcan and Donogh and Malachy were all at Cahermacon on that afternoon. They were all having a meeting about what to do about Gabur.'

'Don't interrupt,' said Ninian severely, aping Flann's manner. 'How can I arrange my thoughts if I keep getting interrupted?'

'Just shorten it a bit,' advised Aidan. 'We haven't got all day.'

Ninian glared at him, but the others were all nodding. They had to tell Mahon everything they had found out, but the sooner it was done, the sooner they could all discuss it.

'Very well, then,' said Ninian. 'Motives and opportunities for everyone:

'Brendan — First motive: he wanted revenge. Second motive: he wanted to marry Eithne and get Lorcan off his hands. He was at Cahermacon, only fifteen minutes' walk from here, about an hour before sunset.

'Finbar — wanted to marry Gabur's girl, Nessa. Gabur hit Nessa with a stick (we'll tell you all about that in a minute, Mahon). He was also at Cahermacon an hour before sunset.

'Nessa — hated Gabur, loves Finbar. Gabur hit her and threatened to tell her father, who would probably have beaten her, that she had been kissing Finbar. She was also at Cahermacon.

'Donogh — hated Gabur, who was trying to get him out of his nice easy place at Drumshee with kind students who help him whenever they can use it as a chance to get away from their law studies. He was at Cahermacon an hour before the killing.

'Eithne — hated Gabur, who had shamed her. She was at Cahermacon an hour before the killing.

'Lorcan — hated Gabur. You should have heard him talking to the master. He started yelling all sorts of words which I won't repeat in front of Ita — but believe you me, he nearly had a fit. He was foaming at the mouth. I think he might have hated Gabur worse than anyone else. Anyway, he was also at Cahermacon.'

'And these are the suspects,' said Diarmuid.

'And then there's me,' said Mahon bitterly. 'Motive and opportunity: I had them both.'

'And, of course, there's Ciarán,' said Aidan lightly. 'He had the opportunity: he had plenty of time to get to the Clab after he left us. By the way, he's admitted that he was lying when he said he saw you, Mahon.'

'And he's mysteriously missing his sling,' added Fergal.

'Yes, but did he have a motive?' asked Ninian.

There was a moment's silence while everyone thought hard.

Eventually Ita shook her head sadly. 'I can't think of any,' she said regretfully.

'It's a pity, though,' said Ninian. 'Ciarán's only thirteen, and the law says that no one under fourteen bears responsibility for an illegal act. Ciarán would be a good one to find guilty. We don't really want anyone to suffer for Gabur's death — let's face it, whoever it was did us all a favour; we just want to get Mahon out of trouble.'

'What about me?' asked Ita. 'I'm only thirteen as well.'

'You didn't have the opportunity,' said Ninian seriously. 'We were all together in the kitchen-house when Gabur was murdered.'

'I wonder if it'll ever be solved,' said Mahon hopelessly. 'I might have to stay here for the rest of my life.'

'No, you won't. My father wants to get it all sorted out during the next few days,' said Ita, cheerfully. 'King Carthen is coming to Coad in two days' time, for the last day of the winter festival. The King wants the case to be heard that day. You heard my father say that at Gabur's burial.'

'Why don't you come to Coad with us tomorrow, Mahon?' asked Cathal. 'The brehon won't be there, and I don't think Owen will be either.'

'What about Ciarán? Or Colm?' said Diarmuid dubiously.

Mahon was shaking his head. 'No, I'll stay here. I'm very sleepy. I couldn't sleep for the last two nights, because I was so cold that I had to keep moving around. I'll sleep tonight, and tomorrow I'll think about everything you told me.'

'I'll come and see you in the afternoon,' said Ita. 'I'm not too keen on all those races and hurley matches. I'll look at all the stalls and the storytellers in the morning, and I'll come back here just after noon. My father will think I'm still at Coad, so he won't wonder where I've gone. I'll bring you some honey-cakes from the festival. The rest of you can come over when you're finished at Coad, and then we'll all go back to Drumshee together.'

Chapter Eleven

The first day of the midwinter festival was bright and sunny, and shortly after dawn the sun melted the frost on the pathways and the roads. The six students of the Drumshee law school set off on their ponies, with baskets holding their lunch slung from the ponies' sides. They were all cheerful and excited. The three days of freedom made a wonderful treat in their busy, hardworking lives, and Gabur's death had removed a great shadow from them all.

'Let's have a walk around first, and then we can decide what to do,' said Cathal happily. 'I love Coad at festival time.'

Fergal had been right: Coad was full of people, and most of them were strangers. There were stall-holders selling all sorts of goods: pots, buckets made of alder wood, shields, knives, swords, horseshoes. There were men selling horses, or practising for the horse-races later on; there were jugglers tossing coloured balls in the air and catching them so neatly that Ita felt almost dizzy watching them; there were storytellers telling the ancient tales of cattle raiders and of magical shape-changing into swans and ravens; there were women selling hot honey-cakes; and in one corner, there was a large crowd of people standing around a tall man dressed in flowing white robes, with a long silver stick in his hand.

Chapter Eleven

Ita left the boys looking at the knives and joined the crowd around the man with the white robe. He seemed to have great power over the people. Everyone listened to him in silence.

'My name is Patrick,' he was saying as she came up. 'I was brought to Ireland as a slave when I was only a boy. I looked after sheep on the mountains in the north of your country. Now I have come back to teach you all about the one true god. The gods you worship — the gods of the wells and the streams and the rivers and the woods; the sun god, the god of light, the god of strength — these are not true gods; there is only one true god.'

~

'And he said,' Ita told Mahon afterwards, when they were sitting in his cave and eating honey-cakes, 'he said that there was only one god, but the one god was three people.'

'Like a triple god,' said Mahon, swallowing some mead. He looked quite cheerful today. Ita had told him about the meeting at Malachy's house and about her father's investigations of what had happened after the meeting.

'No,' said Ita, frowning slightly as she tried to remember exactly what the strange man had said. 'No, he said they were three separate people. He explained it like this. He picked up a shamrock — you know what that looks like? The little green plant that grows on the pathway down the hill from Drumshee.'

'I can't remember,' confessed Mahon. 'There are so many different plants around.'

'Look, I'll draw it,' said Ita. She picked up a stick and drew a large three-leafed shamrock in the dry limestone dust of the cave floor. 'Patrick explained it like this. He said that it looks like there are three leaves, but it's really only one, because they're all joined together to make one big leaf. And it's like that with his god: there are three people, a father, a son and a holy spirit, but only one god.'

Mahon looked at the drawing obediently, but he didn't seem very interested.

'I'm explaining it badly, but he was very interesting,' said Ita. 'He talked about a lovely place called heaven, where his god lives and where good people go when they die. And he said that one of the people in his god came to earth and lived with ordinary people, but they killed him by nailing him to a big wooden cross. After he died, he came back to life again, and then he went back to heaven and his friends started a new worship. Patrick talked for ages and no one moved, they were all so interested in what he was saying. You might be able to hear him for yourself. My father might have discovered who murdered Gabur by now; maybe you'll be able to come back to Drumshee and go to Coad with us all tomorrow. Patrick is going to stay until the last day. He wants to tell the King about his god.'

'Ita,' said Mahon, 'I've been thinking while I've been here. Even if they find out who did the murder, I don't really want to go back to Drumshee. I'll never be a lawyer. I haven't the right sort of head. I can't remember all those laws.'

'What would you do, then?' asked Ita, troubled. She couldn't imagine Drumshee without Mahon.

'I'd like to be a farmer,' said Mahon. 'Maybe

someone would take me on as a farm-boy. Eventually I might be able to get some land for myself.'

'Would that work out?' questioned Ita dubiously. 'You might be an old man by the time you made enough money to buy your own land. And ...' She hesitated and then went on, 'You might want to get married and have your own children.'

'I want to get married, all right,' said Mahon, his ears showing dark red through the rough brown hair. 'I want to get married and ...'

He stopped again, staring intently at the picture of the shamrock which Ita had drawn on the dusty floor of the little cave.

'My grandfather might die, and then the lands of the kin-group will be shared out. I might get a share,' he said eventually, but he spoke in an absent-minded way and his attention was still on the picture of the shamrock.

'Yes, but your grandfather is still quite strong and healthy. He might live for another twenty years,' argued Ita. 'You don't want to wait that long, do you?

'Do you?' she repeated, after a few minutes.

'Ita,' said Mahon, 'I was just thinking, looking at this shamrock — maybe the caves are like this. Maybe these caves here on the edge of the cliff aren't two separate caves, but parts of a big cave — just like the three bits of the shamrock aren't separate leaves, but parts of one big leaf. It makes sense, really, that there would be other caves joining on to this one. There are lots of caves over near Poulnaboe. Ciarán told me that they join together. I think the river going underground could have something to do with it; maybe it carved them out of the limestone. Limestone is very soft.'

'Let's explore, then,' said Ita, getting to her feet.

They wandered around the cave, peering into cracks and climbing over fallen rocks.

'Doesn't seem to be anything,' said Ita eventually. 'Let's go back and have some more cakes and mead.'

'Wait a minute,' said Mahon. 'You see that willow growing at the back there?'

'Isn't that the end of the cave?'

'I thought it was, but that doesn't make sense. A tree needs light to grow. The roof must have fallen in, or something. There might be another cave behind there.'

They pushed their way through the thick bush. There seemed to have been a rock-fall at this spot — lots of them, including some recent ones, judging by the churned-up state of the earth. There didn't seem to be anything else there, though.

'That one must have fallen recently,' said Mahon, pointing. 'Look, it's quite wobbly.'

He touched the large rock, and then jumped back hastily as it started to roll forward. Ita gave a slight scream and jumped back as well.

The rock rolled all the way down the cave and stopped on top of the drawing of the shamrock. They followed it with their eyes until it was still, and then glanced at each other with relieved smiles.

Ita saw Mahon's eyes look over her shoulder and widen suddenly. She whirled around. Behind her, just where the rock had stood, was a gaping hole. Beyond it was another cave.

Chapter Twelve

The new cave was very dark. Ita took a few steps into it and stopped. Her heart stopped as well, and then lurched sideways in a way that hurt her. In the silence, she could hear her breathing, loud and fast.

'Mahon,' she whispered. 'There are spirits from the Otherworld in there.'

She didn't look at him. She kept her eyes fixed on the strange white shapes, but beside her she heard his breathing stop and then start again, fast and irregular as her own. He put his arm around her.

'Mahon,' she said in a terrified whisper, 'there are hundreds of them.'

Her eyes were getting used to the darkness, and she could see more and more of the strange shapes — some of them standing, tall and narrow, on the cave's floor, others hanging down from its rocky ceiling.

'Wait there,' said Mahon suddenly.

He took his arm from around her and moved forward. Ita shut her eyes with dread, and then resolutely opened them again. Holding her breath, she saw Mahon stretch out and touch the nearest shape; and then she heard him laugh. It was a rather cracked, high-pitched laugh, but it was a laugh.

'They're stone,' said Mahon. 'They're just shapes made from stone. Let's go back and get the lantern and look at them properly.'

Ita followed him. She felt weak at the knees. She didn't really want to go into that strange cave; she wanted to stay there in the fresh air, just talking about the future — Mahon's future, and perhaps her own. Mahon, however, had pressed ahead of her and was already on his knees beside the leather bucket they had brought the day before.

'Ah, here it is,' he said with satisfaction. 'A brand-new candle in it, as well. Good old Fionnuala! Now where's my tinder-box.... There we are — lit first time! That's the first time I ever managed to strike a light on my first try!'

He's talking a lot to cover up the fact that he was so nervous, thought Ita, well used to boys and their need to appear brave all the time. I wonder if he really wants to go back into that cave.

'Let's stay here, Mahon,' she coaxed. 'They could be spirits from the Otherworld, really. They might have been turned into stone by a shape-changer.'

A sudden thought struck her, and she gasped with horror.

'Mahon, I've just thought,' she said. 'That cave could be the cave that leads into the Otherworld! Remember that story the bard was telling at Coad at the Samhain festival?'

Mahon laughed. 'What about your Patrick, then? Didn't he tell you that there's only one god — there are no spirits, no Otherworld beyond a cave, just heaven where all the good people go? Come on, Ita, let's just have a look. It's beautiful in there, as beautiful as any heaven.'

It was beautiful. By candlelight, the shapes in the cave glowed with a soft golden sheen. Trembling slightly, Ita stretched out her hand and touched one:

it was wet and slightly gritty to the touch. It seemed to be made of a very soft limestone. Now that she was near them, the shapes didn't look like people; they were more like tall spears, slightly ribbed and pointed at their tips.

The cave was huge; it seemed to stretch back for miles.

'Let's go down to the end,' said Mahon.

'What if we get lost?' said Ita.

'We won't get lost,' said Mahon confidently. 'It's just a big room. You can see to the end.'

It did look quite safe, especially when Mahon held up the lantern and showed Ita how high the ceiling was. She was glad of that. Since she was a young child, she had always hated going into small spaces, hated anything too close to her mouth.

'Let's walk down,' said Mahon. 'Isn't it fantastic? Look at all those pillars! It's like the dwelling-place of the greatest king on earth.'

'Or like that story about Hy Brasil, the magical island out in the western ocean,' said Ita. She had always loved those old stories. She lingered beside an immensely tall spear of limestone, gazing up to its pointed top. It must be the height of ten men, she thought.

'Look, there's another room through here!' called Mahon. 'Just through this passageway. Come on, Ita, I'm going to have a look.'

Ita delayed for a moment, stroking the rough, pitted surface of the limestone. When she turned around, everything suddenly seemed darker. She could no longer see Mahon's lantern; and, worse still, she could no longer see the entrance to the small cave where Mahon had spent the last two nights. Of course, she thought in a panic: the sun has moved around. The cave faces north-east, so there wouldn't be much light coming in; it must be almost sunset, and the sun sets directly behind the cave's entrance.

'Mahon!' she screamed. 'Mahon, where are you?'

'Are you? ... are you? ... are you?' The echoes bounced her words back to her, mocking her terror.

'Mahon!' she shrieked again. 'Come back!'

'Back ... back ... back....' called the echoes, and the sound seemed to have a note of despair in it.

'Here,' came Mahon's voice; but that, too, set the echoes flying around the cave. 'Here ... here ... here ... here....' The sounds came from every side of the cave.

Ita screamed. It sounded as if a herd of wild animals was coming at her from every direction. She cowered down on the floor, afraid to move, pressing her hands over her ears and straining her eyes to see where Mahon had gone.

'I'm here,' said his voice behind her. 'Sorry, I thought you were with me. Are you all right, Ita? Those echoes were great, weren't they?'

'Great,' said Ita shakily. She got to her feet.

Mahon took her cold hand in his own warm one.

'Keep holding my hand,' he said. 'We don't want to get separated. You weren't frightened, were you? Come on. The other room looks even better.'

'Mahon,' said Ita, 'it'll be sunset soon. We'd better get back.'

'Just one look, and then we'll go back,' he said. 'Come on. It's perfectly safe.'

They had to bend almost double to get through the passageway, Ita noticed with a sinking heart. She concentrated on looking ahead at the light which Mahon held in his hand.

Chapter Twelve

Her foot skidded under her and she almost fell.

'All right?' asked Mahon, and his voice boomed off the rocks in the narrow passageway.

'Yes,' said Ita breathlessly. 'My foot slipped on something. Hang on, I'll pick it up.'

When they reached the next cave, Ita saw that it was also full of those strange pillars and spears of limestone. It was wetter than the other cave; here and there, water dripped from the roof and made cloudy puddles on the floor.

'I wonder if these caves go on and on,' said Mahon. 'What have you got there, Ita?' he added.

Ita held up the thing that she had skidded on and looked at it curiously by the light of the lantern.

'It's a sling!' exclaimed Mahon. He stared at it, his face flushed with excitement.

'You know what this means, Ita?' His voice cracked in the middle of the sentence.

Ita said nothing. For some reason, the sling set off some memory in her mind, but she couldn't think what it was.

'Don't you realise?' exploded Mahon. 'I was right! Whoever murdered Gabur did it from the cave. He came right in here. I thought that rock looked like it had just fallen. You must go back to Drumshee and tell the others about this. I think we should bring your father out here. That sling changes everything.'

The sling, thought Ita. It's something about the sling itself. That's what's in my mind. I've seen that sling, or something about it is familiar....

'Whose sling is it, Mahon?' she asked.

Mahon shrugged his shoulders. 'It could be any-one's,' he said. 'It could belong to Brendan, or Finbar, or Lorcan. I don't suppose it belongs to Nessa or

111

Eithne. They wouldn't have slings.'

'They might,' said Ita promptly. 'I have one. I don't bother with it now, but I used to like it when I was younger, remember? I was quite good with it, too — better than Ciarán, anyway.'

As she said 'Ciarán', the memory suddenly came back to her.

'Mahon,' she said, so excited that the words came tumbling out of her mouth, 'Mahon, yesterday when we were coming here, we met Ciarán. The others were teasing him and pretending that they thought he killed Gabur. They searched his pouch to see if he had a sling, and he said he didn't, and then Cathal said, "Yes you do. You showed it to me once. It was made from ram's hide, and it had a patch of white hair on it." Look at that sling, Mahon. It has a patch of white hair on it.'

'And it's ram's skin, as well,' said Mahon, holding the sling up to the lantern and examining it carefully. 'Did Ciarán say where he left his sling?'

'He said he'd left it at Caherblonick, in the herb garden,' replied Ita, 'but, of course, he was probably lying. He wouldn't be likely to say that he left it in a cave just above the Clab.'

'So it was Ciarán, then?' said Mahon slowly. 'It was Ciarán who murdered Gabur.'

'I don't understand,' said Ita, bewildered. 'Ciarán? Aidan said, "He had the opportunity: he had plenty of time to get to the Clab after he left us." But why would he do it? He would have to have some reason for it, wouldn't he? No one kills a man without a good reason, unless it's in a battle or a raid or something. There must have been some reason for Ciarán to kill Gabur.'

'And if he didn't, what's his sling doing here on the floor of the cave?'

They stood there for a long time, just looking at the sling with its patch of white hair.

'I wonder why he came so far back,' said Mahon thoughtfully. 'There was no reason for it. Surely he would have been safe in the first cave.'

Ita said nothing. She cast an anxious look over her shoulder at the darkness beyond the lantern's little circle of light.

'Mahon —' she began. Then she stopped. Mahon had a look of excitement and determination on his face. He was examining a large footstep on the wet ground, near one of the limestone pillars.

'Ita,' he said, 'what was it that Ciarán said to Gabur? You remember — the time when Gabur gave him the piece of silver for being so clever?'

'What? Oh, I know what you mean — when he gave Gabur the feverfew for his headache and told him that foxglove seeds can kill a man. Do you think Gabur was planning to murder someone, and somehow that person heard about it and murdered him first? Is that what you're thinking?'

'Let's go,' said Mahon, ignoring her questions. 'Let's go down here.'

'Shouldn't we go back and get another candle, and put it here, so we'll know this is the way out?'

'Oh, come on,' said Mahon impatiently. 'Don't let's waste time. I'll tell you what I'll do: I'll leave my pouch here. I'll hang it over that bit of rock, and then we'll know that's the way out.'

He took her hand. 'Come with me, Ita,' he said. 'Now I know exactly what happened on the day when Gabur was killed.'

Chapter Thirteen

Ita stared at Mahon. Suddenly he looked years older, almost a man. She left her hand in his and together they moved forward, down through the next cave.

This cave was even more beautiful than the one before, filled with tall spears and dangling swords of petrified limestone. Ita, however, had no eyes for them now. Time and time again, she glanced at Mahon's determined face and at the sling that hung from his wrist. It was Ciarán's sling — she had no doubt about that; but Ciarán? Would he ever have had the courage to murder a man? And why on earth should he murder Gabur?

A sudden thought struck her.

'Mahon,' she said, 'where does Ciarán come from? Who are his kin?'

'What on earth do you want to know that for?' asked Mahon, without slowing his rapid walk down the centre of the cave.

'Well, do you know?' she insisted.

'They're from somewhere over by Liscannor, I think,' he said after a moment. 'Wait a minute — let me think.'

They had come to the bottom of the cave, and they had a problem. There were two exits, one leading to a cave on the right-hand side, the other to a cave on the left.

Chapter Thirteen

'Which way is Poulnaboe, do you think?' asked
Mahon. 'You know, the place where the Fergus comes
above ground again. Think....'

'Left,' burst simultaneously from both of them.

'Good,' said Mahon. 'That should be right. I'm
sure Poulnaboe is slightly north of the Clab.'

He set off down the left-hand cave at a tremendous
pace. This was a smaller cave, small and rocky, with
an uneven floor.

'What were you asking me? Something about
Ciarán?'

'Well, I just wondered,' said Ita breathlessly, 'could
Ciarán be Gabur's son, his unacknowledged son, like
Lorcan is?'

'I wouldn't think so,' said Mahon indifferently.
'For one thing, Ciarán doesn't look a bit like Gabur.'

Why else would Ciarán murder Gabur? thought
Ita. And, after all, I suppose Ciarán could look like
his mother.... But she was too breathless, and too
occupied with keeping her footing on the broken
rock, to question further. Mahon seemed to know
what he was doing, and she followed, keeping a
tight hold of his hand.

The cave forked again, and again they took the left
fork. This was a very low cave, and they made slow
progress. Ita gulped in great lungfuls of air, telling
herself that she was only imagining that the air smelt
stale and stuffy.

The ceiling of the cave grew lower and lower, and
the cave got narrower until they could no longer
walk side by side. They were forced to get down on
their hands and knees. Mahon dropped Ita's hand
and crawled ahead, and Ita crawled behind him. She
could see very little now — only a faint gleam from

the lantern, reflected off the wet rock on either side.

Finally, when she could bear it no longer, she said, 'Mahon, I'm frightened. I hate this.'

'Hang on a little longer,' said Mahon, his voice echoing off the narrow walls of the passageway. 'I think I can smell fresh air.'

Ita took a great, hopeful gulp of air, but all she could smell was the dry, dusty, choking smell of old hay from Mahon's cloak. She swallowed hard, but the lump in her throat seemed to be stopping her breathing.

The passageway got lower. There was hardly room for Mahon. He was going more and more slowly, his wide shoulders turned slightly to fit into the narrow passage.

I'm going to faint, thought Ita. I feel just like I did that time I fainted when I broke my leg. Her face felt burning hot, then icy cold. In a panic she reached out and tried to grab the end of Mahon's cloak, but he moved forward, out of her reach. She shut her eyes and slumped forward.

Ita had often had a dream where she seemed to be falling into a bottomless pit; only at the last moment was she able to jerk herself awake. For a moment, she thought she was in her own bed at Drumshee, having that dream. Then, slowly, she realised that she was lying on the wet floor of a cave. Mahon was pouring gritty, lime-tasting water from his cupped hands over her face, saying her name over and over again in a panic-stricken voice.

'Ita — Ita, are you all right? Ita?'

Ita sat up cautiously. She felt weak and tired and very cold.

'I thought you were dead,' said Mahon. 'You gave

me a terrible fright. I'd just got out of the passage-way, and I looked behind and you weren't there.'

'Where are we?' asked Ita. There was a roaring in her ears. I must still be feeling faint, she thought.

Mahon looked excited. 'If I'm right, we're just by Poulnaboe,' he said. 'Come on. Are you well enough?'

Ita got to her feet and followed him. The roaring sound lessened as she went through the cave. It wasn't a very beautiful cave — just an ordinary, wet, smelly one — but the ceiling was high, and she could see light at the far end. Air rushed towards her and she began to feel a lot better.

At the far end of the cave, Mahon pushed past a clump of willows and held back the branches for Ita.

'There you are,' he said triumphantly. 'We're at Poulnaboe.'

Ita followed him out and stood beside him. It was wonderful to be out in the fresh air again.

'Look,' he continued. 'Look down there, towards the south. That's Caherblonick down there.'

Ita's eyes followed the direction of his pointing hand. She could see the fort of Caherblonick and the newly disturbed earth of Gabur's grave outside the rampart.

She nodded. 'That's Caherblonick,' she said. 'So the caves all join up underground. I wonder if Ciarán knew that.'

'The question is,' said Mahon, more to himself than to her, 'did he come out here, or is there a better way? Let's have a look. It won't be sunset for a while, and anyway, we've got plenty of candle left in the lantern.'

Turning, he went back through the screening bush of willows, into the cave.

'That's the way we came,' he said, pointing. 'That's the entrance to the passageway. Lend me your head-band, Ita, and I'll put it on the rock here, so we'll see it when we come back. Now let's try this passageway here. It leads down towards Caherblonick. This might be what I'm looking for.'

Ita hung back. The last thing she wanted to do was go down another passageway. Once again she could hear the roaring in her ears — at a distance, but still there.

'Do you want to stay here?' asked Mahon. 'I'll just be a minute; I just want to check. Then I'll come back to Drumshee with you and tell the brehon what I think happened.'

Ita shook her head. 'I'll come,' she said resolutely. 'I'll be all right. This passageway has quite a high roof.'

It did have a high roof; and, to Ita's relief, it didn't get any lower. They went down it quickly and easily.

'It ends just here,' said Mahon over his shoulder.

Then he gave a low whistle. In front of them was a door — an ordinary wooden door, its frame set into the rock of the passageway.

'There you are,' he said. 'I bet this goes into the underground room in Caherblonick.'

'I'm sure you're right,' said Ita. 'That's under the house, isn't it?'

'I am right,' said Mahon, his voice rising with excitement. 'I'm sure of it. You see what this means, don't you? There's a way to get from Caherblonick to the Clab without anyone seeing you. That's what he did. He came down here, slung the stone at Gabur, killed him, and then went back this way.'

'So Ciarán did it, after all?' questioned Ita. She still couldn't believe it.

'Ciarán!' exclaimed Mahon. 'Not Ciarán. Why would he murder Gabur? No, it was Colm.'

'Colm!' said Ita, her voice squeaking with astonishment. 'Why should he murder his brother?'

'I was puzzled too,' said Mahon. 'But, you see, the fact that Ciarán's sling was used doesn't mean that Ciarán was the one who used it. Colm could easily have picked it up from wherever Ciarán left it. Ciarán was so excited about the silver piece that he left his sling on the wall of the herb garden. Then Colm came out after talking to Gabur. Remember what you told me? Ciarán said they were shouting at each other.'

'Yes,' said Ita slowly. 'I remember now. Ciarán said they quarrelled, but I didn't take too much notice; Gabur was always quarrelling with everyone.'

'Yes, but then I was thinking about Gabur getting excited when he heard that foxglove seeds can kill a man — so excited that he actually gave Ciarán a silver piece. That couldn't have had anything to do with the feverfew; we all use feverfew for headaches. And then, remember, Gabur went straight indoors to see Colm, and Ciarán heard them shouting at each other. And I thought maybe Colm made a mistake sometime and gave a patient some foxglove seeds by mistake, and Gabur was taunting him about it. And then I remembered about their father. Remember, he died very suddenly? Gabur went to stay with Colm, and Owen taught us for a few days.'

'I remember,' said Ita. 'And Fionnuala was very surprised to hear that Colm and Gabur's father had a bad heart. "I saw that man climbing up the mountain at Mullaghmore only a few days ago," she said to me that evening.'

'And do you remember something else Fionnuala said to you, that day when Gabur was buried? About Colm's father? I was standing beside you, so I heard what she said.'

'Yes,' said Ita eagerly. 'She said, "He was a wicked, cruel old man, just like Gabur. He led his poor wife a dreadful life, and when she died, he carried on tormenting Colm." Do you think Colm killed his own father because he couldn't bear him any longer?'

'Yes,' said Mahon solemnly. 'And you know the penalty for *fingal*, the murder of a kinsman?'

'Banishment from the country and the tribe,' said Ita, in an awestricken whisper. 'Oh, Mahon, if you're right, Colm has committed the crime of *fingal* twice.'

'He is right,' said a voice. 'He's right, but I don't think there's much he can do about it.'

The door beside them opened and a man appeared in the doorway, holding a wicked-looking knife in his hand. Mahon made a quick gesture as if to take his own knife out of his pouch, then dropped his hand. Of course, thought Ita, he's left his pouch at the entrance to the cave —

In that same instant, the man grabbed hold of Ita's long plaits and pressed the knife to her throat.

'Very clever,' said Colm. 'You worked that one out very well. My brother was wrong about you, Mahon: you're a clever boy. Now don't try to get away, or to do anything to me. If you do, I'll cut Ita's throat. Come in here, both of you. In you go, Mahon. You go first. Put the lantern down there, on the floor of the passageway.'

Chapter Fourteen

It was a small, dark room that Colm pushed them into. A few glowing pieces of charcoal burned in an iron basket in the centre of the floor; their faint light showed a damp clay floor and rough, lime-washed stone walls. Still keeping an arm around Ita and the knife at her throat, Colm took a candle from a shelf, lit it from the fire in the basket and placed it inside a horn-plated lantern that stood on the shelf. Now they could see everything very clearly: the bunches of drying herbs hanging from the ceiling, the walls lined with shelves covered with pots and small platters, the rough wooden table bearing a stone pestle and mortar for pounding herbs.

Colm reached out an arm and lifted a little pot, full of small black seeds, from the top shelf.

'You were right, Mahon,' he said quietly. 'These are foxglove seeds, and I did kill my father with these. Look around you. I keep all my dangerous medicines down here, and I am the only one who has the key to the two doors. See, that's hemlock there, and that's monkshood, and that's mandrake, and that's ivy. Any one of these can kill a man.'

Ita gazed at him in horror. He had always seemed to be such a gentle, kind man. Had he been secretly murdering people with his medicines for a long time?

'No, no,' Colm said, seeming to understand her thoughts. 'These plants do no harm if they're given in tiny doses. A minute amount of foxglove seeds is good for a failing heart, and a small portion of boiled ivy berries is good for the brain-sick. No, the first person I ever killed was my father, and I bitterly regretted it.'

He stopped and looked away. Ita could see that there were tears in his eyes.

'For months afterwards, I used to wake up at night sweating with the horror of what I had done. I had killed my own father in a fit of rage! And when I did sleep, I kept having nightmares about being put out to sea in a boat with no oars — the terrible thirst and starvation, and eventually death.... I kept thinking about taking some hemlock and killing myself, but I was too much of a coward.'

'And then?' prompted Ita. If only we can keep him talking, someone might come, she thought. The other boys know I'm at the cave; they might come looking for me. They might see the signs that we left.

'Why did you kill Gabur, then?' she asked softly and sympathetically. Was it her imagination, or had Colm's grip on the knife slackened? She looked at Mahon and saw his eyes alert and his body tensed, like a cat about to spring on a bird.

'Did Gabur guess?' she added, desperately trying to keep Colm's attention away from Mahon.

'Not straight away, no,' said Colm.

Yes, thought Ita, the knife has definitely moved. It was the flat of the blade, not the sharp edge, which was against her throat now. She made an encouraging noise.

'I began to think that no one would ever know,' continued Colm. He seemed glad to talk about it; the words poured eagerly from him. 'No one liked my father much, anyway. There was no one to mourn him. Even Gabur was glad he was dead. We divided the land between us; Gabur got the best portions, but I didn't argue. I didn't deserve anything. It was just so wonderful to have peace in this house. I began to think that I might get married, even — have a family of my own.'

Mahon had taken a cautious step forward, but Colm hadn't noticed. Still he went on talking, in an almost dreamy way.

'He treated me so badly, you know. He was never like a father to me. He treated me like a dog; he shouted at me, threw things at me. He was always making me do things for him — I could never sit down without him finding some task for me....

'One evening I came home dead tired. I'd been out all day, I was exhausted, I was soaking wet, and I still had to make some medicine for an old man with a weak heart before I could rest. I made my medicine — pounded up the foxglove seeds — and I was just going to my room when he shouted to me to bring him some hot mead.'

The knife had dropped down to the level of Ita's chest. Colm's eyes were looking gloomily into the glowing charcoal in the iron basket. Mahon took another step forward.

'I heated the mead, and then I came back down here, ground up some more foxglove seeds until they were a fine powder, and tipped the powder into the mead. I added some more honey so he wouldn't taste the bitterness. Then I gave it to him. He drank it, and very soon his heart stopped. He was dead.'

Ita stole a glance at Mahon. There was only the iron basket between him and Colm.

'It was that fool Ciarán,' said Colm bitterly. 'He
started it all. As soon as Gabur heard about the foxglove seeds, he put two and two together. He told
me that when he came to see our father's body, he
found some small black seeds on the pillow. I suppose
they must have fallen off my tunic; I was so tired that
night that I didn't know what I was doing. Anyway,
he accused me of killing the old man, and he said he
was going to see the brehon after he visited Nessa's
father at Drummoher.'

From the corner of her eye, Ita saw Mahon's foot
slowly come out. Colm began again, talking very
quickly:

'I knew what I had to do,' he said. 'I knew I had to
kill him. I could go through the caves and just wait
until Gabur passed along the Clab. Then I could kill
him and go back the same way. No one would ever
know. I'd be safe. I sent Ciarán over to Drumshee
with a message, to get him out of the way. After he
went, I saw his sling on the wall of the herb garden.'

Suddenly Mahon kicked the basket of burning
charcoal over Colm's boots. Colm gave a start and
tried to kick the basket away; Ita wrenched herself
from his grasp; Mahon's fist came out and knocked
Colm to the floor. Mahon grabbed Ita's hand. They
both hurtled through the door. Mahon slammed it
shut behind them, picked up the lantern and ran,
dragging Ita with him.

They had only gained a minute, however: almost
instantly they heard the door open again, and Colm's
footsteps were pounding down the passageway
behind them.

'Quick,' said Mahon, swerving violently around a
bend in the passageway.

'Oh!' exclaimed Ita. Her foot had caught in a long fold of her cloak. She fell forward heavily, bumping into Mahon. There was a dull thud as the lantern was knocked out of his hand against the rocky side of the passageway. Instantly the candle inside the lantern went out, and they were left in darkness.

The thud of the lantern had sent the echoes flying again, and behind them they heard Colm's heavy footsteps falter and then stop. He was listening, listening for their footsteps. Of course, thought Ita; he can't see anything either. He was following the light of our lantern.

Mahon placed a hand over her mouth and they crouched there, listening. Then they heard Colm's footsteps — not coming nearer, though; he was moving away from them, back to the underground room at Caherblonick.

Maybe he's going to go away, to escape, thought Ita hopefully. Perhaps he was going to leave them alone, mount his horse and ride away and avoid the trial at the King's court of law.

'Gone back for a light,' whispered Mahon, very softly, in her ear. 'Come on. Go quietly.'

Keeping close to each other, they groped their way through the blackness of the passageway. Ita began to feel the sense of panic coming over her again. She couldn't see the roof of the cave, and she didn't know how close it was. The air seemed to smell old and stale.

Quickly she glanced over her shoulder, and she was almost relieved to see a pinprick of light behind them. Mahon was right: Colm had gone back to fetch a light. He was not going to let them escape him as easily as that.

'In here,' whispered Mahon, pulling her into an opening in the side of the passageway.

I don't think we came this way, thought Ita. The pinprick of light had vanished, but she could hear the sound of Colm's footsteps booming off the rock. He was running, running as fast as he dared on that uneven, rocky ground.

The footsteps grew louder. They were coming nearer and nearer — and then, to Ita's relief, they passed by. They went on down the passageway, slowly becoming fainter.

'Come on, we'll keep going this way,' whispered Mahon.

Ita followed, but her ears strained for a sound from the main passageway. Is it just my imagination, she wondered, or are those footsteps getting louder again?

It wasn't her imagination; Colm was definitely coming back. He had realised his mistake. He must know these caves and passageways very well, thought Ita; he's guessed that we turned off.

There was a loud roaring in her ears. With a start, she realised that it wasn't the beginning of that terrible faintness; it was the sound of water tumbling over rocks. They must be quite near to the River Fergus.

She looked back. The light was still behind them — no longer a pinprick, but a soft glow which lit up Colm's running figure. He could see his way, while they had to fumble through the darkness. He was going faster than they. Soon he would catch up with them. That one glance had been enough to show Ita that he still held his knife in his hand; the light had shone on the gleaming blade.

Suddenly Mahon stopped.

'Ita,' he said in a terrified whisper, 'the river is coming in.'

At that instant, Ita was almost swept off her feet by the flow of the water swirling around her ankles. The only thing that saved her was Mahon's iron grip on her wrist.

'It's a flood!' he shouted, above the thunder of the water. 'It's been raining so much, these last few days, that the Fergus must have burst out of its usual passageway. It's flooding all the caves. I can feel a ledge here, above us — quick, Ita, climb up!'

By now the water was sweeping past at knee-height. Ita reached up. Mahon was already above her, still holding her wrist. They climbed as rapidly as they could, moving around a corner in their climb; and then, to her incredulous joy, Ita saw a faint glimmer of daylight far above them. There was light coming in from the outside; and where there was light, there was air.

She was no longer afraid. 'I'm all right,' she shouted. 'I've got a firm grip. Let go of my wrist. See if you can get a bit further up.'

At that moment, there was an agonised scream. For a second, a pinprick of light danced on the surface of the roaring torrent which filled the cave below them; then it was extinguished. By the dim light from the opening above them, they could see a body twisting and turning in the flood. Then it was gone, washed away in the blink of an eye.

'Mahon,' screamed Ita, 'he'll be drowned!'

'We can't do anything,' Mahon shouted back. 'We'd be drowned ourselves if we went down there. Come on, Ita, climb! The water is still rising.'

It was a difficult climb up the wet, slippery, near-vertical side of the cave. Mahon and Ita had spent much of their childhood climbing trees and rocks, but this was more difficult than anything they had ever done.

The river must rise to this level sometimes, thought Ita. The rocks are covered with moss, and they're soaking wet.... Inch by inch, they edged their way up, Mahon leading and Ita following, testing each handhold and foothold before she put her weight on it. They were both panting heavily and Ita had a painful stitch in her side.

'Ita,' came Mahon's voice, 'we can't go any further up. The rock-face juts out here. We'll be killed if we try to go on. And we're really near to the opening, too! If we could just find a way around this bump, we'd be out of here in no time.'

'Let's rest for a while,' said Ita, almost thankful that they could go no further. 'This ledge is big enough for both of us to sit on. Maybe the flood will go down as quickly as it rose.'

'Not much chance of that, I'd say,' said Mahon. 'Remember all the rain we've had in the last few weeks? I'd say all the water has been flowing down from the mountain and getting stored up in some deep cave, and now it's burst out. Maybe all of the caves are flooded. Our only hope is to get out by that opening up there. I wish I had my pouch with my tinder-box and flint.'

'There's some sun coming in now,' said Ita. 'That opening must face south-west. Look, it's lighting everything up.'

It was true: they could see everything now. The river was still rising. The black water swirled dangerously near them, though they were still a good arm's length above the flood. All around them, the rock bulged out; its surface was smooth, with no handy holes or ledges. They sat there, looking around, trying to find some way to escape.

The minutes went by slowly. We must have been here an hour, thought Ita. The sun's rays grew weaker and weaker. They no longer shone into the cave; only a faint pink light showed in the top of the opening.

'It'll be dark soon,' said Ita hopelessly. Her cloak was soaking wet up to her knees, and she had begun to shiver.

'We'll have to sit it out for the night,' said Mahon. 'We'll have to keep each other awake. It'd be too dangerous to go to sleep; we might fall. Don't worry, Ita,' he added, and she could hear in his voice the great effort that he was making to be cheerful and courageous. 'Don't worry. Once morning comes, the flood water will probably have gone down — after all, we've had no real rain this week, so the flood can't get any worse — and then we'll climb down and make our way back. At least we're in no danger from Colm now. No one could come out of that torrent alive.'

Ita shivered, partly from the cold and partly from the horror of it all. She moved closer to Mahon, and he put his arm around her.

'Don't be upset,' he said gently. 'It was a better end for him than a trial and the shame and that horrible death. He must have drowned in an instant.'

'How did you guess it was him, Mahon?' asked Ita, trying to put the thought of drowning — of choking in that icy water — out of her head.

'Well, the first thing that made me think of him

was that footprint in the cave,' explained Mahon. 'Up to then, I'd been thinking about Ciarán, because of the sling, and because I was sure that the caves would connect up with Caherblonick — but Ciarán? It just didn't make sense. But then, when I saw the footprint, I knew it was a man's — Ciarán has small feet, about the size of yours. Then, suddenly, everything rushed into my mind.'

'And you asked me about the foxglove seeds.'

'Yes. You see, I remembered that Gabur was smiling when I saw him, and he always smiled when he was about to torture someone. I remembered that Gabur and Colm had been shouting at each other, and I wondered what they quarrelled about; and then I remembered about their father, and how he died suddenly. And I remembered that on the night Gabur died, when Colm gave me something to make me sleep, he came into our room before any of the rest of you, and woke me; and he kept asking me if I'd seen who killed Gabur. And yet, afterwards, he pretended to believe that I'd done it. All of these things came back to me, and it all began to make sense. It was like a game of chess — all the bits came together, and suddenly I could see the solution.'

'It was very clever of you,' said Ita. 'If we ever get out of here, you'll be able to claim the King's reward.'

'I'd forgotten about that,' said Mahon slowly. It was quite dark now and Ita couldn't see his face, but she could hear the excitement pulsing in his voice.

'We'll get out,' he said confidently. 'We must! I'm going to start shouting. We'll take turns. They must be out looking for us by now. It's been ages since sunset; the others must have discovered that you're missing, and they'll have gone back to Drumshee and told everyone. Your father must be beside himself with worry about you.'

They took it in turns to shout. For a while it was quite interesting — they made a game out of it, counting how many times the echoes repeated the word 'Help' — but then their throats began to get sore. There wasn't the slightest glimmer of light from the opening above them, so they couldn't tell if the flood waters were beginning to go down.

'The water doesn't seem as noisy any more,' said Mahon hopefully.

'That's probably because we're getting used to it,' said Ita. She felt close to despair, and she knew her voice sounded as if she was going to burst into tears.

Mahon held her even closer and kissed the top of her head. 'Ita, would you ever think of marrying me?' he asked.

'I might,' said Ita, startled out of her misery. She thought about it for a moment and felt herself smiling in the darkness. She would be like Nessa, who would probably soon be betrothed to Finbar. She would be married. Mahon may not be as good-looking as Finbar, she thought, but he's a lot braver and more dependable.

'Yes, I'd like that,' she added.

'You would!' Mahon's voice was exultant. He took his arm from around her and stood up.

'Help!' he yelled, in a roar that was louder than any river torrent.

'Mahon! Ita!' came back a voice — a voice which was usually quiet and low, but which now sounded like the notes of a giant horn.

'Father!' screamed Ita.

'We're down here!' shouted Mahon.

The next moment, the blackness of the opening above them was filled with the light of lanterns and flaring torches.

'Hang on,' came Brendan's bull-like voice. 'We're sending down ropes. Hang on — you'll be fine now. Just wait there, Ita; your father is coming down on the rope.'

Hardly able to believe that they had been found, they watched as, hand below hand, Flann swarmed down the rope, landed on the narrow ledge and took Ita in his arms.

Mahon went up first. He was as agile as a squirrel, and he swarmed up in a moment. Then two ropes were sent down; Flann tied one around Ita's waist and hoisted her up the first few feet, and then she felt herself being tugged up. She tried to help by swarming the way Mahon had, but her muscles were cramped from the long, cold wait on the ledge, and in the end she just let herself be pulled up. A minute later Flann followed on the second rope. He had always been a great rock-climber, and he came up almost as quickly as Mahon had.

Everyone was there at the top of the cliff, Ita saw, once she had disentangled herself from her father's arms. There was Brendan, the mighty cords on his arms still standing out from the effort of pulling the rope; there was Finbar, with Nessa nestling against him; there was Lorcan, his face covered with sweat, but lit by a joyful grin; and there were Fionnuala and old Donogh, and all the students from the law school. Even Ciarán was there.

'We saw your pouch, but we couldn't go any further because the caves were filling up with water,' said Diarmuid.

'So we went back to Drumshee to get help,' added Fergal.

'Brendan was telling us that there were a lot of potholes,' chimed in Ninian. 'We had got the ropes and everything when ...'

'I came and told the brehon that the underground room was on fire and that Colm had disappeared,' said Ciarán smugly.

'And Colm? What happened to him?' asked Flann, pulling on his lawyer's robe, which he had taken off for his climb down to rescue Ita.

'Oh, Father!' said Ita. 'Colm's drowned. He was swept away in the flood. And ... and Colm was the one who murdered Gabur. Mahon guessed it all. Gabur found out that Colm had killed their father with foxglove seeds, and he threatened Colm that he was going to tell you when you came back. Colm followed him — he went through the caves from Caherblonick — and slung a stone at him with Ciarán's sling, and then escaped back underground.'

'She's raving, the poor lamb,' said Fionnuala.

'No,' said Flann thoughtfully. 'She's not raving. It all makes sense. I did wonder, that first night, the night when Gabur was killed. Colm seemed very anxious to pin the murder on Mahon, while trying to make sure that he didn't suffer any penalty because of it. Well done, Mahon. I always did think you were a clever boy. Now let's get you both home and into dry clothes. You can tell me the rest tomorrow.'

'And, Father,' said Ita, 'Mahon will get the reward from the King, won't he? He was the one who found out who murdered Gabur.'

'I'll talk to the King about it tomorrow,' promised her father.

'Will I get a reward?' asked Ciarán.

'Your reward is to be thrown down the hole into the cave,' said Aidan.

'Oh, leave him alone,' said Mahon, yawning deeply. 'After all, if he hadn't mentioned foxglove seeds, I would never have guessed.'

Chapter Fifteen 🌸

They all slept until late the next morning, and by the time they arrived at Coad it was swarming with people. Everyone was buzzing with excitement, and everywhere they went they heard the name 'Patrick' and the strange new word 'baptism'.

'What's happened?' Flann asked an elderly man.

'The King has become a Christian,' he replied. 'A lot of other people have as well. See the big crowds over there, around the man in the white robe? They're all being baptised. He pours water over them, and that makes them into new men.'

'That's the man I was telling you about,' said Ita to Mahon. 'That's Patrick over there.'

Mahon nodded. He had had a bath and washed his hair, and he wore a new cloak which Fergal had lent to him. Diarmuid had lent him a gold brooch to fasten the cloak, and Fionnuala had scrubbed his tunic to a state of snowy whiteness. Mahon would be the most important witness in the lawcourt, and the whole of the Drumshee law school was determined that he would do them credit.

The court began at noon. King Carthen sat on a high, flat rock covered with sheepskins, and the people grouped around him, some sitting on rocks or on the ground, some standing or lounging against walls. There must be at least two hundred people here, thought Ita.

Her father stood beside the King, and the students of the Drumshee law school clustered around him. There would be no races or other amusements until all the cases had been heard.

'Oh, no,' whispered Aidan. 'It's Malachy and his neighbour and the boundary stone again. I don't think I can bear it. That stone will be dizzy if it keeps getting moved around like that!'

The others giggled as silently as they could, pressing their knuckles into their mouths. Malachy and his neighbour had been engaged in boundary warfare over a piece of valuable, well-drained lime-stone land for as long as anyone could remember. They were forever accusing each other of moving the stone. This time there was clear testimony from two witnesses that Malachy had been seen moving the stone, and King Carthen, on Flann's advice, dealt with it briskly. A fine for Malachy — the same sum as his neighbour had been fined a few months before. The two men nodded at each other, fairly amicably, and the case was over until the next moon-less night, when the stone would be moved again.

Then Gowlaun the blacksmith was accused by his neighbour Cian of letting his bees trespass all over Cian's meadow and paying no compensation for their trespass.

'I don't believe it,' whispered Ita. 'Is he serious?'

Ninian nodded, his narrow, clever face alight with interest.

'There is something in the judgement texts,' he whispered back. 'I've never heard of a case, though.'

'What sort of flowers did you have out in your meadow at the time?' asked King Carthen, showing more interest than he had during the previous case.

'Meadowsweet, my lord.'

'Excellent honey, meadowsweet honey,' pronounced the King, visibly licking his lips.

'He seems to like honey. You should've sent him a pot before your case came up, Mahon,' whispered the irrepressible Aidan.

'Hush,' said Ninian angrily. 'I want to hear what the brehon says.'

Ita noticed that Owen was looking puzzled, but Flann was not at a loss.

'My lord, the judgement texts say that the owner of the bees must pay for their trespass with a pot of honey.'

King Carthen nodded. 'That seems fair. Is it good honey?'

'The best, my lord,' said Gowlaun glumly, and then added reluctantly, 'You might wish to sample some, my lord. I'll send you a pot.'

The King beamed happily, and Aidan dug Mahon in the ribs. Mahon was taking no notice, however. He was fiddling with the brooch on his cloak and licking his dry lips. Flann had got to his feet again, and Mahon knew that the last case of the day — the case of the unlawful killing of Gabur the lawyer — was about to be heard.

'My lord,' said Flann, 'last Saturday evening, Gabur the lawyer was murdered by a blow from a stone to the back of the head. In the beginning it was not known who had done it, but my student Mahon saw Gabur walk along a path, and saw the stone hit Gabur on the back of the head. Mahon saw no one else, but he realised that the stone must have come from high up on a cliff behind Gabur. He found a small cave there, and deep inside it he found a sling.

He recognised the sling as belonging to Ciarán, the apprentice of Colm the physician, Gabur's brother. At first Mahon thought Ciarán might be responsible for the murder, but he could find no motive. Then Mahon and my daughter Ita, his fellow student at the Drumshee law school, explored the cave and found that it stretched for a few miles underground, from the spot where Gabur was murdered back to Colm's dwelling-place.'

'Wait a minute,' interrupted the King. 'Let the boy speak for himself.'

Mahon came forward, his face pale. King Carthen smiled at him encouragingly.

'I first thought of Colm when I saw a man's footprint in the cave,' began Mahon. 'I was fairly sure that the cave must lead back to Caherblonick, and I guessed that that was how the murderer must have escaped, but the footprint was too big to be Ciarán's. Then I remembered that Ciarán told us that Gabur was very excited when he heard that foxglove seeds can kill a man, and that he went in and talked to his brother Colm straight away, and they quarrelled. And I remembered that no one had expected Colm's and Gabur's father to die of a bad heart, so I thought Colm might have done it.'

'Wait a minute,' interrupted the King. 'This is all very clever, but can you prove it? Colm is dead, drowned in the flood in the cave, and I hear that he confessed that he was doubly guilty of *fingal* — that he killed his father and his brother — but how can we know for sure? We have to take your word for it that he confessed.'

'There is also my daughter Ita,' said Flann. 'She was with Mahon, and she heard what Colm said.'

Ita's heart gave a lurch and she gulped. She had not expected this.

She looked at Mahon's white face and resolutely got to her feet. She had to do her best for Mahon. The King had to believe him and give him his reward, give him the chance to lead his life as he wanted.

Slowly she walked forward and stood beside Mahon, in front of King Carthen.

'Well, Ita,' said the King, smiling at her pleasantly.

This is my first time speaking in a court of law, thought Ita. It won't be the last, though, so I'd better get used to it. Briefly she envied her father his ease with the King and all the people around the court. Then she took a deep breath and let her mind sort through all the confusion of the day before.

'Colm told me and Mahon that he killed his father because of his deep anger at the bad treatment he had received from him,' she said clearly, her voice steadying after the first few words. 'He told us that he killed Gabur because Gabur had guessed that his father was murdered with foxglove seeds — Gabur had seen some of them on the bed just after his father died — and he was going to tell the court of law that Colm was guilty of the crime of *fingal*. Colm couldn't bear the thought of disgrace and exile and, probably, death.'

'And he told you both all of this?'

Ita nodded. 'I think he was going to kill us. He had a ... a knife in his hand.'

In spite of her good resolutions, her voice broke as she remembered the danger they had been in. Mahon moved closer to her, so that his shoulder touched hers. She dug her nails into the palms of her hands and took a deep breath.

'Mahon saved us both by kicking over the fire-basket. We ran down the passageway to the caves, and Colm ran after us; but then the water flooded into the caves and he was swept away. He definitely confessed to the two murders, but that was only after he had heard Mahon explain to me exactly what had happened,' she ended firmly.

'Then Mahon will receive the reward of ten ounces of silver,' said the King, rising to his feet and speaking loudly so that everyone could hear. He turned to Mahon with a smile. 'Will you save it and open up your own law school later on?'

Mahon shook his head. 'No, my lord,' he said. 'I want to be a farmer. I'll use it to buy some land.'

'In that case,' said the King, 'I will give you that piece of Gabur's land which was his own property, inherited from his father. There are no near kin now that the two brothers are dead, so I will give you the land near Lough Fergus — land fit for seven cows. You can keep the ten ounces of silver to stock your land with cattle.'

'Thank you, my lord,' said Mahon. He bowed low. Ita heard a stifled giggle from the other students behind them, but Mahon took no notice.

'And now,' said King Carthen, 'we can let the horse-racing begin.'

Flann moved to the King and murmured to him.

'Oh, yes,' said the King. 'I had forgotten. First there are other injustices to remedy. Lorcan, the son of Eithne, will also receive some of Gabur's property. There seems little doubt that he was Gabur's son from the time when Gabur and Eithne lived together. Brendan will receive back the money that Gabur owed him.'

There was a quiet murmur from the people standing around. Every face looked satisfied, Ita noticed, and several heads were nodding. The King rose and moved away, followed by the crowd.

The students of the Drumshee law school clustered around Mahon.

'So now everything is just perfect,' said Ita.

'Perfect,' echoed Mahon. He had a flush on his cheekbones and looked excited and nervous. He looked around at all his friends and then quickly took Ita by the hand.

'Let's go and see your father,' he said.

When they found him, Flann was standing by Patrick, listening with his usual courteous attention. He hadn't been baptised, Ita noticed; there was no mark of water on him. He wouldn't be easily swayed from the beliefs of his forefathers, she guessed.

He saw them coming and moved away from Patrick and his followers.

'Well,' he said to Mahon, with his usual keen look, 'are you content?'

Mahon nodded.

'In some ways, you would have made a good lawyer,' mused Flann. 'You are clear-minded and intelligent. Your memory would always have been a problem, though. I think you've made the right decision. You will have to talk to your father, but I think he'll look at you differently now that you're a man with money and land behind you. If he agrees, then you will cease to be a law student and become a friend — a friend to me, and to my daughter,' he added, with a quick look at Ita.

'Master —' said Mahon, and stopped. 'Sir,' he amended, and again he had that look of having suddenly grown years older. 'I'd like to be more than a friend to Ita. I would like to marry her.'

Flann shook his head decisively.

'No, Mahon,' he said. 'You're both too young. I don't like those early marriages. Give yourself time, and give Ita time. You'll have to learn your farming, build your house and set yourself up, and she has her studies to go on with. Be friends for a few years, and then think again. You may both think differently then. In the meantime, Mahon, you must go on living at Drumshee until you build your house. You're a brother to all the students and a foster-son to me, and you'll stay that way. Now go back to your friends and let me talk to Ita.'

When Mahon had gone away, looking bewildered and yet still excited, Ita didn't know what to say. Is Father right? she wondered. She didn't know what to think. Did she want to marry Mahon, or to carry on at the Drumshee law school?

In a way, she realised, she wanted things to carry on as they were; she just wanted Mahon to be still part of her life.

'You'll see him every day, you know,' said Flann, as if he could read her thoughts. 'It will take him quite a while to get everything right on that land by Lough Fergus. There's no dwelling-place on it; Mahon will have to build one. It will be best for him to live with us, where Fionnuala can go on cooking and washing for him, for at least another year. That will give you both a chance to decide what you want.'

Ita nodded. Maybe it's best, she thought. Mahon and I will stay friends, best friends, and then after a few years maybe we'll get married.

'Did you get baptised? Did Patrick baptise you?'

she asked. She didn't want to go on thinking about marriage at the moment. She would talk to Mahon afterwards and see how he felt.

Flann shook his head. 'No,' he said. 'I think I'm too old. But I have a feeling that this new idea might be here to stay. Your children will probably be Christians; maybe you will be as well. Who knows?'

'I'd like to keep the goddess Brigid, though,' said Ita. 'I like going over there and making little offerings to her. Maybe I could keep her hidden under the big ash tree and no one would mind.'

Flann laughed. 'Keep your goddess Brigid,' he said. 'She's been a good friend to our kin. Now go and join your friends. Enjoy the fair. Now that the lawcourt is over, I can enjoy myself as well. I think I'll go and look at the horses. Oh, by the way, Finbar has got his appointment as horn player to the King. The King heard him play this morning and granted his wish.'

'So Nessa will be getting married soon, then,' said Ita, feeling a little jealous.

'Early marriage suits some girls,' said Flann. 'You and Nessa are two very different people. Finish your studies, and then we'll see. Look, the lads are over there; why not go and join them? They seem to be having fun, judging by the noise they're making.'

The boys were all in high spirits when Ita joined them. Cathal was sitting on Mahon's chest, thumping him and shouting, 'Go on, Mahon, tell us — will you be an *ócaire* or a *bóaire*?'

'A *bóaire*,' said Mahon.

'Wrong,' said Cathal. 'He'll be an *ócaire*, won't he, Ninian?'

'Yes,' said Ninian. 'An *ócaire* is a farmer with seven

cows. Your honour-price will be three *séts*, or one and a half ounces of silver, or one and a half cows.'

'I can buy ten cows with my ten ounces of silver,' argued Mahon, pushing Cathal off his chest. He stood up and brushed down his tunic, which was no longer so snowy white. He had taken off Fergal's new cloak and Diarmuid's brooch, Ita was glad to notice.

'You won't want to spend all your silver on cows, Mahon,' she said. 'You'll need to keep some to build your house and things like that.'

'And you can use some to pay your friends for teaching you the law,' added Cathal.

'You never taught me anything,' said Mahon heatedly.

'Let's teach him now,' yelled Cathal, who seemed to be in a mad mood. 'Come on, Mahon, what's the honour-price of a cow?'

'What's the honour-price of half a cow?' screamed Aidan, dancing around and around Mahon.

'Or of a bee?' shouted Fergal. 'What's the honour-price of that bee that trespassed on Cian's meadow?'

'Or of half a bee?' yelled Diarmuid, howling with laughter and punching Mahon on the arm to make him share the joke.

In a moment they were all wrestling on the ground again — like a crowd of five-year-olds, thought Ita. But she couldn't help laughing. Suddenly fear, hatred, suspicion and murder seemed to melt away into a gloriously warm feeling of fun and companionship.

'Come on,' she said. 'Let's have some mead and some honey-cakes, and then we'll go and watch the horse-racing.'